BEFORE

ALSO BY JOSEPH HURKA

Fields of Light

BEFORE

JOSEPH HURKA

Thomas Dunne Books
St. Martin's Press 🕮 New York

This is a work of fiction. All of the characters, organizations, and events portrayed in this novel are either products of the author's imagination or are used fictitiously.

THOMAS DUNNE BOOKS.
An imprint of St. Martin's Press.

Grateful acknowledgment is made for permission to quote from *The Poetics of Space* by Gaston Bachelard, translated by Maria Jolas, copyright © 1964 by The Orion Press, Inc. Original copyright © 1958 by Presses Universitaires de France. Used by permission of Viking Penguin, a division of Penguin Group (USA) Inc.

www.thomasdunnebooks.com
www.stmartins.com

Design by Gregory P. Collins

Library of Congress Cataloging-in-Publication Data

Hurka, Joseph.
    Before / Joseph Hurka.—1st ed.
      p. cm.
    ISBN-13: 978-0-312-35990-4
    IBSN-10: 0-312-35990-X
    1. Cambridge (Mass.)—Fiction. 2. Psychological fiction. 3. Suspense fiction.
  I. Title

PS3608.U768 B44 2006
813'.6—dc22

2006052193

First Edition: May 2007

10 9 8 7 6 5 4 3 2 1

For my aunt,

MIROSLAVA HŮRKOVÁ

and for my father,

JOSEF LEOPOLD HŮRKA

In the manner of men of the past
We build within ourselves stone
On stone a vast haunted castle.

—VINCENT MONTEIRO
Vers sur verre

BEFORE

PROLOGUE

Bohemia, June 9, 1942

The boy is tall and strong, all of fourteen. He hikes late at night through the forest, breaking the Nazi curfew, on an errand for his mother. He feels the heaviness of the clothes and curtains his mother has repaired through the straps of his rucksack.

He steps over the dark earth. There is the smell of the rugged pines, the sound of kestrel birds, the pale flight of them. Wind moans in the trees. The moon, silvered by clouds, is a ghost behind the shapes of branches.

Where the forest ends he enters a field; tall grass brushes at his knees. There ahead are the darkened Krušina farm buildings—everything is dark now, after nine P.M., under the Nazi penalty of death; Jiri Posselt pauses and looks carefully at the barn he approaches. He sees no movement, no shapes of Wehrmacht soldiers: no glow of a cigarette. Still he waits; after a few moments there is a sound, at first an insistent humming, growing louder into engines, coming from the direction of the farmhouse. It is a dark scraping of planes.

Jiri steps back and crouches in the forest, watches the old stone house against the hill, above it the white ghost of moon. Clouds twist over that light, and then three Messerschmitts emerge from the rise, flying very low, pin lights on their wings. They come on fast and steady, a quick moment of growing, thunderous engines, a quick run of shadows stretching over the field. Jiri feels the power of them in his throat and chest, in the bones of his arms and legs. They disappear behind the trees, the scraping following them.

He waits to make sure he does not hear the engines coming around, growing louder again. When he cannot hear them anymore he rises and walks purposefully across the grass to the first barn. He steps inside the rolling door; it has been left slightly ajar. The building is a great, yawning space, and in the shadows horses shift at his entrance. He can smell them and the hay, the old wood and mortar of this place. He stays in a dark triangle a moment, until the horses have settled, until all he can hear is wind tugging loose shingles above, twigs scattering. To his left in the darkness is a clean, lidded hutch, and Jiri opens it and takes out milk bottles, eggs, cheese, bread that is still warm. He sets all of these on the floor, then slips off his rucksack and pulls from it the bundles tied in burlap, the curtains held firm, wound around stiff cardboard, and puts these inside the bench. He loads the food into his rucksack, eggs on top; folds the excess cloth of the rucksack closed, fastens the straps.

He glances out the door: a battered path here through weeds, oak branches shifting on the charcoal sky. Still no shapes of men, no movement out in the field. It is not likely the Nazis would be patrolling this far out of town; in the two years that Jiri has been running the errands to farms outside his village he has been caught only once, and that was by a Czech gendarme, who whispered at him, fiercely, to get the hell home. Jiri swings the rucksack onto his shoulders, closes the lid of the hutch quietly.

He goes into the night. Soon enough the trees of Bohemia sway over him again, and the song of cicadas pulses through the darkness. He keeps up a steady rhythm, his shoes finding their way over roots and packed earth. At times he walks in a blackness so complete he feels he might be a ghost, a spirit sailing close to ground. The thought of this, and the greater danger of patrolling troops as he gets closer to town, frightens him. He imagines Nazi police discovering his form against the trees. There would be dogs, flashlights. The white of guns firing, the impact of 9 mm bullets. How much of this would he feel? How long would he be conscious of the Nazi bullets ripping into him?

He forces himself away from the image: He thinks of his family. His father, once a science teacher, a lover of the stars, would tell him to look for the archer, Sagittarius, coming up over the next open field; Jiri imagines the bright constellation, the drawn bow. He imagines his mother, how just ninety minutes ago she checked her list carefully to make sure she had packed everything she had sewn for the Krušinas; Jiri's sister, Helena, cleaning the kitchen counters, laughed at their mother's precision. Helena will be eighteen in two days' time: Jiri can think of this. He has bought her a bracelet that is in safekeeping in his parents' room. He showed it proudly to his mother when he purchased it, and she exclaimed over its bright blue and red hand-painted swirls, its gloss of varnish. His mother said, *Helena will like it so much, honey, what a wonderful gift.* Jiri hears his mother's voice in his head, sees her hands turning over the bracelet. Helena admired the bracelet in a shop in Plzeň, on a day when Jiri was impatient to get to the soccer fields, and he smiles in the darkness at how his sister will kiss him and remember it.

Now the clearing ahead. But the growing rumble of more planes comes from over Jiri's right shoulder. The moon is momentarily bright, lighting the forest floor. Jiri ducks into a group of fallen trees, glances up in the overwhelming sound as the monsters hurtle through the branches. Arados this time: soaring over the pale field, three planes tipping to follow the phone lines, their pin lights disappearing into the dark.

What is all this, tonight? There has been more military activity everywhere since the Resistance attack on SS General Heydrich's car, and particularly since the Butcher, as he was called, died from his wounds five days ago. Heydrich was Hitler's Bohemian ruler, his enforcer; now more Nazi guards patrol the mine in Kladno, where Jiri and his father work: more of the Messerschmitts and Arados fly overhead. There is a new, brisk feeling even with the soldiers who have been wounded on the Russian front and who are billeted in Jiri's small village, in the Sokolovna gym. A Nazi lieutenant used to come on crutches to watch the Sunday village soccer games—his heels had been blown off on the Russian front. He was an old German track star who enjoyed telling sports stories with the youngsters, but since the Heydrich killing the lieutenant does not come down from the Sokolovna anymore.

Jiri watches the sky carefully before he steps into the field. The planes are gone, their sound fading. The telephone poles are stout and the lines are tight against the heavens. Jiri, standing there, looking up, feels the earth beneath him spinning. He looks down again, shakes his head, regains his balance. He adjusts the rucksack into a more comfortable position, then follows the phone lines into one more dark forest. The ground dips and rises. His footsteps are a hushed progression; now through the last trees he sees the valley fall away and the hayfields pale yellow and there, below him, his village: a collection of pastel buildings, their rooftops angles against violet and gray. The baroque onion steeple of St. Martin's Church hovers just beyond the granary. To the west, only a few hundred meters from him, is the old Sokolovna, the moonlight breaking over its red pastel walls. He will circumvent it and the soccer fields by staying above in the tree line, then drop down through the hayfields to the Horák farm, to the path that leads to his home on Andělu.

Then Jiri hears the truck engines. He drops quickly to one knee, his heart pounding. When he looks long and hard at the dark village streets, he can make out hulks of German trucks—many of them—moving slowly. He inches back up the slope to a small stand of poplars, eases off the rucksack and sets it beside him, and, lying on the ground, propped on his elbows, he stares at Spálená Street, the main thoroughfare. The moon comes out of the clouds and he can just distinguish the rectangular vehicles slowing and stopping near the granary. Soldiers, dark spots, descend onto the cobblestones. Others already surround his village; he can make them out now, sometimes in groups, moving like shadows in the hayfields below him. There are so bloody many of them! The highway, too, far to the left, is filled with the shapes of trucks. Jiri smells the grass and dirt beneath him, feels the wowing of his heart in his ears.

The boy lies in the forest. He listens for any sound that might tell him what is happening with his mother and father and Helena. He hears the cicadas and the truck engines; the moon slips behind a parade of clouds and his village becomes dark.

At least, by now, his family will know that he's seen the Germans, that he will have the sense to stay away. He thinks: *If the*

Germans are rounding up citizens for questioning, they soon will know that I am not among the others. They will get records from the Town Hall. His mother will say that he is overnight in the mine barracks. But how long will it take before they check with the Kladno mine and find out that he is not? And what will that suggest? What will happen to his family then?

He will wait here, hidden, until the Germans have done whatever they came to do—a search only, he hopes, *please God,* and then over. There is a girl down there named Marie Příhodová that he has been seeing lately. He thinks of her now at her window, looking out at the soldiers, her eyes wide with fear, calling back to her family. A few days ago, at that wall on Spálená where the German trucks have lined up, he held her under those oak and willow trees. He remembers the sound of her voice close to his ear that evening; how they stayed there, holding each other, in their dark village. The smell of her hair. Now she, now his family, now his friends, are watching the Nazi troops from their windows, and Jiri's throat tightens and he can hardly swallow.

There is sweat beneath his hair and at his neck. Sometimes he puts his head down on his forearms. His eyelids are eventually so heavy that at two in the morning he cannot help falling into a restless sleep. *He is in the village church, and Christ hangs against the stained glass windows; he is a child and impetuous, and his parents are admonishing him. His best wool suit itches; he wants to be out, running free with his friends on the endless green, the fresh-cut grass smell, of the soccer fields. Helena is trying to keep from laughing at him, her eyes alight at his antics, and then her face turns in shock to a sound.*

It is a gunshot, and Jiri is awake. The crack echoes over the fields. Jiri can hear the faint screaming of a woman. He swallows, getting up again on one knee near the trunk of a poplar, watching, straining to see anything beyond the few shapes. In the field below the Germans stand, implacable dots, every few meters. Two distant rifle shots are fired almost simultaneously, and there is wailing from women and children. Jiri curses, clenches and unclenches his fists. The onion steeple is growing more distinct, and the steep church roof becomes dark red; a megaphone says something fast, unintelligible. Jiri looks at his watch: It is four forty-seven. How could he have slept so bloody long? The hours at the mine have drained him lately. Still, he should not have let it happen. He works his hands together, rubs his head with his fists, alternates between crouching and rising to watch the village. He stares desperately at the church.

What is his sister doing now? Are her eyes in fear, and are the Germans pushing her and his father and mother this way and that with their rifles? The thought of it makes him rage. And what about Marie—has she been ordered into the street in the morning, as the Nazis tear apart her home in their search for Resistance equipment? Birds flutter above him, sail over the lightening gray valley. He stares at the rooftops, wiping his face with his hand, closing his eyes, trying to think of something he might do. But every alternative puts him in the hands of the Nazis, too, gives his family, Marie, the horror of seeing him captured, probably shot.

Someone is in unimaginable grief down there; perhaps it is he, Jiri, who should be in grief. There was a funeral in town a few weeks ago, for old man Bříza, the grocery owner. Jiri thinks of the carriage that bore the coffin, the clopping of the horses, the glossy, varnished wood of the hearse reflecting the cobblestones, and how as the procession went through town wounded German soldiers watched, many of them on crutches, smoking cigarettes, their eyes

distant or indifferent; Father Steribeck led the long line of mourn-
ers up to the cemetery. Jiri remembers the sad but defiant procession as they turned against the sky; the wife and three sons at
the grave, the stillness of them, the leaves of the willows and
poplars trembling.

The muted bell of St. Martin's Church rings five times. A group
of trucks leaves the village, moving quickly down the highway. Jiri
sees the low trail of dust behind them. There is a barricade on the
road; he watches the trucks slow and then again pick up speed.
The sky is coming in overcast; clouds gather heavily over the few
fading stars. He can smell the wetness of coming rain. The birds
are beginning their chattering.

Then the morning is broken by a volley of gunshots. It seems to
explode with its suddenness and terror inside of Jiri.

He watches from his place in the trees, weeping, his hands in
fists. The sound has come from the southwest, the direction of his
home. Fifteen minutes later there is another volley from the same
place. It echoes and rolls over the small valley.

He nearly runs into the village—*to do what, precisely?* He can
die with his family. That would be something. *No: I will not go in
and die.* He cannot imagine giving that to his mother as one of her
last memories. The thought of him free is probably the last thing
sustaining her now. *If she, if they are still alive.* He weeps, trying to
keep his choking throat silent.

Another volley. Distant, angry shouting of men; Jiri realizes
through his panic that he is not hearing the hysterical sounds of
women and children. Might his mother and sister and Marie have
been in the trucks? Suddenly, he is sure that is the case: The
women and children are being brought elsewhere. He stares at the

black, wet strip of highway, the village, the last, hazy moon and stars overhead.

Father, he thinks.

Another volley. The sky opening on this horror. A scattering of blackbirds and kestrels from the trees. *I should go and die with him like a man.*

He would say no. He would say, Find out what has happened with your sister and your mother, where they have been taken.

A ragged explosion of gunshots. Jiri clenches his jaw and, crying, swings on the rucksack and turns back in a crouch toward the forest and runs: scuttling like a crab, then standing straight, willing his thighs to move, his lungs heaving. Runs and walks and stumbles and runs again, making sounds in his throat of hysterical grief and rage, shaking his head back and forth.

The forest darkens and the rain comes hard and slants through the trees and Jiri hears the *huh huh huh* of his body fighting with each step.

I

ONE

Cambridge, Massachusetts: September 10, 2001

T he pigeons flutter and sail through the city. They light over
the vacant eyes of Demosthenes, high on Memorial Hall;
they swoop beneath the leaves of Harvard Yard and crowd the
rooftops above Massachusetts Avenue. It is four o'clock on a stunning fall day.

In the speech therapy office on Story Street, where shades are
drawn against the late sunlight, Jiri Posselt is writing. He fills in the
ovals that his therapist, Marjorie Legnini, insists upon, these areas
at the top and bottom of the page meant to sharpen and gather his
memory.

Who: Me
What: coming back from the Krušinas
Where: Lidice
When: June 1942

Jiri feels his wife, Anna, and Marjorie Legnini across the circular table, watching him carefully. He can hear the ticking of the

clock over Marjorie's desk, and though he writes with the help of a lamp, Jiri senses late afternoon sunlight hovering on the large fern in the corner; ribbons glow on the rug and partially across Marjorie's desk. The figure *1942* hovers at him, rising from the page as if in conspiracy, but he closes his eyes a moment and thinks of the village at night below him, and when he opens his eyes the hovering has stopped and he is able to lean forward and apply himself again to the writing. He writes for a long time.

Jiri feels then Marjorie Legnini leaning over him; in the shadowed room she has come around the table and is watching his lines, and he feels her nodding and then—a strange series of sounds—she is quiet and then weeping, and Jiri glances up to confirm this—tears trickling down her cheekbone—and he quickly stares down at the page. He's faced a great deal of sentimentality himself since his strokes six months ago, and he is frankly uncomfortable with it; sometimes he will find himself weeping in the shower, beneath the torrent of water, from the smallest goddamn thing—a song heard on his shower radio, a remembered, hopeful face of one of the teenagers down here in Harvard Square, these kids with all their heavy damn makeup and hair every which way and their black clothes, walking about like sad crows. The open weeping has something to do with the way his brain has changed, and when it comes he cannot control it.

Marjorie moves back to her seat again, and Anna puts a hand over those of the young woman. Jiri watches them: Anna in her light blue sweater and with her glasses on her nose, and Marjorie in her white short-sleeved shirt, the lines of wetness beneath her eyes. Anna says: "It is hard to think of all this."

"I've had an easy life," Marjorie says, wiping the back of her hand over her cheek, recomposing herself. "I really see that when I think of what you people went through."

"Well," Jiri says, quietly. He clears his throat, emotional himself, his mouth firm. Marjorie is a good, earnest kid, maybe thirty-two years old, usually fairly jolly, and Jiri always looks forward to the individual and group sessions with her, joking with her, working hard on memory games, on his speech patterns; he isn't quite sure how to handle this, these tears, and is grateful to look up and realize that she has collected herself.

"I don't usually get like that," she says, smiling, her eyes shining.

"It's good," Anna tells her, still holding a hand over one of Marjorie's. "It means you care. Believe me, not all medical people are as caring as you are."

Jiri nods very seriously and then concentrates again on his paragraph. His writing is even and running straight across the page; it does not seem that he has repeated any words. He looks up at his therapist hopefully. "I think I've managed to finish it," he says.

In March, as he was standing at the garage just behind his apartment building, Jiri's vision suddenly turned white; he saw his wife, the blue cinder of the drive, the large sumac bush by the chain-link fence, all becoming pale, disappearing. He said, *My God, Anna, something is wrong.* At St. Leonard's Hospital he was told he'd had a transient ischemic attack—a ministroke; on his second night there, a blood vessel ruptured in his brain and the pressure of the blood damaged his vision, particularly in his left eye. Two months later, still in recovery, he suffered another stroke that left him with halting language. With Marjorie's help his speech has steadily gotten better (sometimes now he gets through one or two paragraphs without thinking about them) and his eyesight is stabilizing, though he has trouble with bright light—it can even be painful—and with the letters piling up and hovering weirdly during reading. His short-term memory, too, is still often uncertain.

Jiri is most comfortable speaking with his wife, and Marjorie Legnini, and his Trowbridge Street neighbor Tika LaFond, a photography student who often takes him walking on their road or at the Arnold Arboretum in Boston. Other people, not as familiar with his condition, are more difficult to converse with; he becomes self-conscious and especially does not do so well on the phone. Often he cannot find the precise word he is looking for, as if there is a trickster in his brain, holding up a cloak before the knowledge he needs. The cloak can make him desperate—he must force himself to slow down and think a word or sentence through, using small tricks of his own. He will bend the right side of his mouth down with concentration and wait for a trigger to the word, as Marjorie has taught him (college helps you for*ever,* replace the "v" with an "m," and *Emer*son is Tika's college; a *hen* would make a nice subject for a painting, so Shelley *Hen*derson's art gallery on Bow Street is the place where Anna has worked for nearly seventeen years). Occasionally Jiri catches himself being sly and clipping off a phrase at an opportune moment, when in truth he had much more to say and knew—a swift panic—he wouldn't get it all out. Sometimes the words just will not come, and Jiri will end his subject abruptly and shake his head with disgust.

There is this thing that passes between Jiri and Marjorie—she picks up on his hope, his will to fight, and they are a good team—

and now she comes beside him again, wheeling over on her rolling stool, looking at his lines, still wiping her cheekbones. "It is a *huge* improvement, Jiri. Here and here"—she points with her finger— "the letters are a little cramped. You see how they bunch up? But the rest of these letters here are quite well spaced."

Jiri nods. "A least it doesn't look like they keep jumping off a diving board anymore."

"Ex*actly*," Marjorie says. "This is progress. I told you, it will go slowly, but surely. And no repetitions, all the way through. First time that's happened since we started."

She wheels over to her desk and pulls something from a drawer. "Look," she says. "See? This was from right after you left rehab."

He does not remember these pages as he takes them from her. He had simply been writing his address for her, apparently, for here is his manic scrawling (could it be? could he have been so screwed up?), reading *39 Trowbridge Street, #5, Cambridge, Massachusetts 02138.* Some of his first efforts were crossed out with great frustration. Marjorie sets these examples next to his more precise writing now, and she and Anna try to encourage him, saying, "Look how far you've come, Jiri." But Jiri's jaw grows tight at the thought of how incapacitated he was, of what can happen to him so suddenly. Marjorie, seeing this, tactfully puts the old writing back into her drawer and takes the Lidice memory he hands to her and places it, chronologically, into the three-ring memory book that Jiri has with him always now, *June 1942* after *September 1933.*

On Brattle Street a few minutes later, walking to the parking garage, Anna's hand is tight on Jiri's arm, guiding him through the crowded sidewalk; he steadies himself with his cane. The memory book is firmly in his other hand. Somewhere there is a smell of fried dough in the air, the sound of someone singing off-key. He wears dark wraparound glasses; still, the sun shining into windows above is too much for him, and he turns his eyes down to bricks, hearing footsteps, voices, all around him. In crowds he must always walk with Anna's help, as if he is some old damn horse.

"All right, Jirko?" Anna says.

Jiri nods, but his wife stops him and adjusts his glasses, which are starting to fall down his nose. "There," she says. "Pretty cool character."

"Still can't see a hell of a lot," Jiri says. The street seems to be punctuated with glowing light: on this passing woman's pastel hat, on the silver buttons of this man's shirt. A group of teenage girls laughs as, to the angry honking of automobiles, they cross the road and go into Wordsworth Books. They have oversize jeans that are torn and scuff the street, and Jiri mutters for Christ's sake that someone should get them some decent pants.

"That's just what the youngsters are wearing, for goodness' sakes," Anna says. "It's the fashion."

"*On je nedbale oblečeny.* It's no good," Jiri says. "Their parents shouldn't let them go out like that. They must be just fourteen."

"That is *old* in this country. Where have you been?" Anna says.

Jiri grunts. He taps with his cane, and they walk again. Two women pass in white chadors, speaking in rapid Farsi. Buildings here have fallen a little into shadow, and Jiri sees more clearly, though if the shadows get too dark his left eye will be blind and his right not much better. There is music nearby, on the brick sidewalk to the left—gypsy guitars and some sort of percussion—and people are gathered, clapping: Jiri and Anna slow down and ease into the crowd. Anna's hand pulls: Some college students, seeing Jiri's slow condition, his large sunglasses, make room. At the center of the gathering acrobats whirl batons of fire against the brick buildings and late blue sky. Jiri must study the scene a moment to take it in. The flames dance with the rhythm, and to Jiri's difficult eyes and brain suddenly look as if they occupy the horizon, a terrifying trembling of fire that constricts his chest. The drums grow louder, and the performers plunge the torches into their throats. Anna exclaims with the crowd, but Jiri leans toward her and says, "Let's go, Anna," his voice hoarse with despair. Anna immediately puts her left hand on Jiri's arm and the college students part, their faces a little bewildered and worried for him, and Anna says, "*Ano,* Jirko, let's go."

It is peaceful, darkly shaded, in their building on Trowbridge Street. Jiri and Anna go up the elevator to their third-floor flat, a place decorated with paintings of Prague: of the Little Quarter or "Venice" area of the city, of Týn Church and the National Theatre and Charles Bridge. There are paintings of the Slovak and Bohemian countrysides, too, and, within a mahogany-and-glass case in the living room, small Bohemian glass jars and figurines, many of these smuggled out by relatives in the straw bodies of dolls during Communist years.

Their daughter, Markéta, newly married and living in a Seattle suburb, stares out with her husband from a photograph on the living room wall. Jiri can see this clearly and he smiles: Markéta is thirty-five now, and he had been quite worried for her—all career and no personal life—until last year. *Time soon for children,* he thinks. He imagines Christmas, small blond Markétas running about him in the flat.

On an end table beside the living room couch is a framed pencil drawing that Jiri once did, with his sister, of his childhood home. In it, you see the back of the family building, tall and thin yellow pastel and with the steep, red clay roofing shingles, and in the garden that is the foreground are large sunflowers beneath the light of the sun. A broken mortar wall is at the edge of the rendering, where Jiri as a boy could sit and read books well into the summer evenings. Jiri, aged fourteen, had done a group of these drawings with his sister, and his mother had given them as gifts to relatives in Prague. He did the pen-and-pencil work, and Helena painted the pieces with bright watercolors.

Jiri walks through his living room now, still clutching the memory book; the last sun dancing through the screened balcony doors takes a moment to organize in his vision. Shards of light from the crystal pieces are an unbearable kaleidoscope, and then finally begin to separate into their respective shapes. He closes his eyes and waits. Anna is in the kitchen: taking herbs from the shelf, opening the oven; roasting sounds, pan sliding and water hissing on the burners. In July, at Massachusetts Eye and Ear, Anna said to him, Ono se to polepší, *it will get better, the doctors say it, Jirko, it is just a matter of time*. He imagines the pocket of blood on his brain, slowly dissipating, allowing his eyesight to return properly. He opens his eyes. The light is still dancing, but not blinding him; it is more pronounced out on the balcony: hardwood slats and ribbons of white. The blond-wood grandfather clock here in the living room is tocking. The doorway into the small library is shadowed, and Jiri steps through it.

Here, books run foot to ceiling, with only an ottoman and lamp and a small table and a window onto Trowbridge Street for companions. Beyond, through the next doorway, he can see the large bed and his desk with his computer, a black, unused brain against varnished mahogany. He puts the memory book on the small library table, straightens. Here are books on the art of translation and many other volumes that he himself has translated into English from German and Czech; histories of the Third Reich and Communism, and prose by authors of Czech and German literature and philosophy—Čapek, Havel, Kafka, Macek, Masaryk, Rilke. There is a section for his own reading and research, detailing the Germany and Czechoslovakia of the past thirty years, picking up from when he left the American intelligence services in Munich in 1969. Two large filing cabinets are built into the shelving, filled neatly with manuals and pamphlets that Jiri has translated for the Boston Guild, the firm that has been his most steady client for thirty years. One entire drawer contains copies of contracts, dating back to 1970, that ensured he would be paid for his work.

When he was hit by the strokes, he'd just finished projects for Michelin Tires and the Pacific World Bank of California—he and Anna thankfully are still getting checks from these jobs. Anna earns a small income at Shelley Henderson's art gallery. Medicare is taking care of medical bills, and the Posselts have found a pharmacy in Quebec where they can order the drugs Jiri needs, in bulk, at one-third of American cost. Jiri hopes that he and Anna shall not have to dig too deeply into their savings for their other responsibilities before he is able to make a decent enough recovery to go back to work. He steps to the ottoman and holds the back of it and looks out the window at the shifting leaves, the shard of Trowbridge Street below, until the feeling of dread sweeping him passes.

His wife, too, has a full section of library wall—books on art, some of these volumes so large that Jiri built a special area into the bookshelves to house them. Above the ottoman, on the only space of white wall in the room, is a framed letter from Václav Havel, thanking Jiri for a 1991 translation of a book of the president's essays.

Jiri turns to the right suddenly, startled. From Robert Payne's *The Life and Death of Adolf Hitler,* an old volume with the glossy spine torn and creased, a white swastika hovers at him in triplet, spins. The spider moves toward him. He steps back, shaking his head. The figure keeps coming at him. He goes into the living room, his cane tapping at the floor angrily. He turns on lamps, and there is a nagging, arthritic pain just below his kneecaps. Jiri paces, closes his eyes, then opens them, grateful for the sudden clarity with which he can see the Oriental rug, the floorboards of wide pine.

He thumps back into the library, his jaw set, and the swastika still hovers, but not as dramatically. *What a goddamn thing, this brain of mine, these goddamn eyes.* He stares the swastika down, tries to make it still; it spins, slowly.

Jiri steps again into the living room, listens to the sounds of his wife. He opens the screen doors and goes out onto the balcony. September evening here, leaves: Trees blacken to his left now nearly into blindness; the air is crisp, cool. He moves to one of the rockers, sits, lets his knees ease from all of the walking. *Close your eyes, just for a bit,* he thinks. *Don't think of the swastika. The more angry you get the more damn confused you get.*

Trowbridge Street lies beneath a canopy of leaves. He can see the steps to Tika's apartment building across the road, the glass window of her door like dark mica. The chain-link fence there is the boundary of Trowbridge Academy, a small secondary school. The leaves whisper around him, making him think that he is in a boyhood tree house. *Close your eyes.* When he closes his eyes the white spider still seems to be hovering at him, against his eyelids.

He tries to imagine other things, but the swastika imposes itself over all memory. Somewhere nearby, as he begins to sleep, there is a sound of wings.

There is a high-pitched cry of birds, the slant of rain through the forest. He runs four days, following the Berounka River, watching the stars. With his footsteps, he repeats the address his father has had him memorize for just such an emergency: Křivoklátská 148, Plzeň, Křivoklátská 148 . . . When he sleeps, once, in the ruins of a castle, he dreams that German shepherds are coming up the slope at him, a few feet away, straining at leashes held by SS soldiers. Helena is yelling a warning at him, Tvůj život je v nebezpečí, Jiří! And he wakes and spits and keeps up his flight, moonlight down the riverbank, water like white knives flickering. His throat tastes of vomit, and it is difficult to swallow; he goes to the river and drinks water and spits and runs again, steady sharpness of pines against the night sky, hears the huh huh of his body fighting. Křivoklátská 148, Křivoklátská 148 . . .

He keeps in the thick trees wherever he can, branches snapping at his face—or he runs in water shallows over small stones. Railroad tracks go along the other shore of the Berounka, and sometimes he watches the Czechoslovak Railways cars hurtle through the night, the dark succession of freight cars, flatbeds coming from the Škoda Works with huge tarpaulin-covered tanks and guns; he listens to the rolling heaviness of wheels on steel.

He finds himself standing in his living room, knees aching. The display case is before him, small Bohemian crystal vases behind glass. He does not know when he got up from the rocker. His eyes focus; his cheeks are soaked. On the end table beyond the couch, in its small, gilded frame, is the picture he drew of his home in Lidice. For a moment he imagines Helena there, in the garden, in the shadows of sunflowers, smiling at him.

But someone has been knocking on the door, and Anna is calling him, anxiously: *"Jirko, podivej se kdo to je."*

His wife comes into the living room, a towel in her hands, glasses hanging from her neck, and now she is before him, looking at him, saying, "Jirko, my God." Looks at his eyes; she touches his face, his wet cheeks, with her cupped hand. She holds her fingers on his jaw and then there is the soft knocking again and Anna turns to answer the door.

TWO

Tika LaFond's roommate, Susan Bristol, is having an affair with a married man she met on the Internet. He is Stuart Livesy, an economics professor from the University of Sydney, who told his wife, legitimately, that he would be attending a conference in Boston. Tika thinks about it now, stepping into her Trowbridge Street apartment; about how she has been avoiding coming home ever since Susan picked Stuart up at Logan four days ago—bending over her photographs in the red light of the Emerson darkroom or working at Standish's Pub in Harvard Square, leading people to tables, handing them menus, taking orders. Usually Susan and Stuart go off to Stuart's hotel room in southern New Hampshire, but last night they were here when Tika got home from work. She could smell marijuana from Susan's bedroom, and she tried to go to the refrigerator quietly for a snack, but they had come out to greet her. Short, smiling Susan with her dark eyes, dark curly hair. Her lover in his late thirties, smiling. *Nice to meet you, Tika. I've heard nothing but good things.* Tika wasn't sure what to say, what to do with her hands, how to act, *like maybe I'm just meeting him for the first time at an art gallery or something and not like they were fucking ten minutes ago?*

The hallway is dim and smells of onions and tomato sauce—Susan and Stuart's recent spaghetti dinner. Tika turns on a lamp: dark paneled wood, a mirror in which she is startled by her newly shorn hair. She has the wide, fortunate eyes, the high cheekbones of her sister, Kascha, though something in Tika's face is not as arresting, she knows—there is a rare *type* of face, determined by mathematical, incremental certainty, that can light up film, sell to humanity; she does not have that type of face. This does not matter to her: she would rather be behind a camera than in front of it. But she has a good face that draws men and the attention of women to her; she is fortunate in this, and she is grateful if her boyfriend, Jesse McKye—a rock musician and salesman at the Strings & Things store on Brattle Street—finds her attractive. The new haircut, close to her head, emphasizes the wideness of her eyes. She brushes her hair back away from her forehead and looks at her eyes a moment, the green-dark of them in this hallway.

Fall coats hang from pegs, and below them she puts Susan's mail on the small table. Bills for Susan: credit cards, Internet service. An *Acoustic Guitar* magazine, an advertisement soliciting funds for the local public television station. The strap of Tika's camera case is heavy on her shoulder, and she shifts it as she looks at her own mail. There is a postcard: Kascha has been working in Rio this week, though Tika is sure that by now her sister has flown back home, to Milan; on the card Christ beckons high over the sea, the city, ocean waves below Him, and on the flip side Kascha has written: *Dear Tike, shooting three days here, a lot of men (mostly Americans) gawking on the beach but the Brazilian men are beautiful.*

*Would take one or two back home with me if I had the time and pa-
tience. Can't wait to be with you in NYC next week. XXXOOO.*

Tika walks into her bedroom and puts the postcard and her bills
and the case and a slip of photographs on the dresser, beneath the
mirror. Above her bed a pencil drawing of John Lennon stares at
her: tired genius eyes behind National Health glasses, jeans jacket,
and T-shirt. Kascha did the drawing in high school—a sketch of
the famous 1968 John Kelly photograph—and Tika has always admired it. Kascha used to do a lot of drawing back then; it was
something their father encouraged and their mother did not, argu-
ing that for anyone to make it in the art world, one had to have *ex-
ceptional* talent, as she put it. There were many crying jags over this
and other judgments, and Tika defended her sister's art, her spirit,
yelling fiercely at their mother while Kascha slammed doors.

Tika has left a hairbrush tossed on the bed, her bed unmade.
She pulls off the coverlet and straightens the sheets tight, tosses
and pulls the coverlet flat, feeling as she does so something ease
within her, an anger she has been holding at Susan all day subsid-
ing, shifting where it belongs, to Susan, something Susan needs to
deal with. It is strange to think about this thing with the Australian
man. Last night, Tika whispered her objections fiercely to her older
roommate in the bathroom, for their landlord's living room was directly above Susan's bedroom: *Don't you think Joe will smell the
grass, Susan?* And Susan cocked her head in the strangest way, as if
Tika were a distant vision, an acquaintance who needed simple reassurance (a new moment for Tika; since they had been living
together—since the moment Tika'd met her after answering Susan's ad—Tika felt they'd always been close. Now, for a brief moment, that was not so certain). Susan had said, *Well, we'll put it out*

then, and the moment passed and she said, *God, Tike, he fucks like a rabbit.* Tika had not said anything to that, but she had imagined the wife at her sink in Australia, peeling carrots, brushing hair back from her forehead with the back of a hand, two children racing by the doorway behind her.

Susan does alumni relations work for Trowbridge Academy now, basically trying to part wealthy alumni from their funds. She goes through many men, but there is something different, something more serious, about Stuart; she touched her chest and couldn't stop smiling when she was preparing to get him at Logan. She kept saying, *Fuck, man, I can hardly* breathe.

In the bathroom Tika pulls down the shade, starts the shower, then undresses, leaving jeans, shirt, underwear, bra, and socks hanging loosely on the large radiator. She steps in and water beats against her chest, her collarbones, a hollow sound; she thinks of Jiri joking two days ago at the Arboretum that he cries in the shower for no goddamn reason at all. He's been a hell of a sport—so courageous, with his wry humor—about everything that has happened to him. Tika holds him by the inside of his bicep as they walk, feeling the lightness of him there, of his bones, the lightness of age, *of the body disappearing.* The colors of the Arboretum, the brightness of mountain laurels and azaleas, seem to swallow them both. There was something—in a moment by the roses—that he had wanted to tell her, his face grave, and then the moment had passed. She'd thought perhaps he'd hit the wall he sometimes does, the inability to go on with his sentences. She'd said, *It's okay, Jiri,* but he shook his head and looked at the ground and Tika didn't press it.

The water comes down now, streaming through her hair. She

feels her face lengthen with the image of Jiri in her mind. She has been dreaming, in fear, of Jiri lately, and a nightmare from a few nights ago comes back to her: She was in an old, crowded theater—dark, timeworn wood and heavy red curtains, searching for her friend, seeing him then a number of rows below, sitting with a man she did not know. The man had dark skin and black eyes; he was dirty, as if from some squalid, violent country with unrelenting sun. Tika was trying to reach Jiri, to warn him, but people were blocking her way. There was something more to the dream, but she cannot remember what it was.

She works in coconut-smelling shampoo, rinses. The water swirls on chrome, the soap falls in quick coils. She conditions her hair; soaps her underarms, her chest, her neck; scrubs with a Seychelles Islands sponge—Susan picked up a bunch of these with another lover just a few months ago. Somewhere in southern New Hampshire Susan is twisting in bed with Stuart. Tika imagines them, the flesh of it, tongues, light on Susan's back, then on Stuart's back; somewhere in Australia the wife now is washing her hands, spraying soap down the sink with the hose. Tika rinses, glad for short hair, for just being able to run your hands through. She shuts down the shower and steps out onto the tightly woven rug. A breeze comes from the window, the shade clicking, the curtains drifting toward her. She takes a large towel and dries herself, rubbing her face briskly.

She closes the lace curtains in her bedroom and turns on a light and puts shaping gel in her hair and smoothes on skin lotion, then combs and dresses carefully: gabardine trousers, cotton shirt, thin black leather jacket, mules; she will be seeing Jesse later tonight, at a gig of his in Central Square. There is the sound of teenagers going by on skateboards on the street just underneath her window, restless thunder. She takes the photographs she has worked on in the afternoon from the Ilford plastic liner and sets them against the wall beside the floor-to-ceiling window. Other photographs are there, in plastic liners or mounted for her semester project—a retrospective of Jesse's band—on archival paperboard. Here is a hand of Jesse on a dark ebony fret board, an eye of the other main vocalist, Elijah. Here a full shot of the band at Harborfest, in June—Eric, the drummer, glancing over his shoulder, smiling at her, and the other four guys looking happily up also. They have just finished a song, and ten thousand people are cheering; there are banners for Miller Lite in the distance. Jesse's hair is tousled black, swept quickly away from his forehead, and his glasses shine in the bright day.

At her bureau Tika slides open a drawer, takes out her white rope bracelet, slips it on. She takes the Leica from a drawer and from a shelf above five rolls of high-speed Kodak film. These she puts in her camera case and swings it over her shoulder. She turns off the lamp by the bed and the hallway lights, retrieves a salad and tomatoes from the refrigerator, and locks the front door behind her. Then down steps and across the street—Trowbridge Street is quiet now, cavernous in this moment of her crossing; a few of the leaves above her are tinged with early color—and up the brief porch at 39. Now there is a sound of a bird protecting territory in the willow beside her: now a faint heavy rap drum, many streets away, a sound that quickens Tika's heart with its promise of violence. Three flights up in the old elevator, the smell of this hallway that of cigarettes and vegetable soup: Tika comes to number 5 and knocks. There is no answer and after a few moments she knocks again. She watches the door open, and here are Anna Posselt's eyes, staring and wet.

"Hi, Anna," Tika says, tentatively. It is strange that her friend is not opening the door farther. "Vivian Topalka gave us too many tomatoes. I thought you could use some."

"Oh, yes. Thank you, honey," Anna says, pulling glasses up to her nose. She reaches a hand out for the bag that Tika holds: crackling paper. The door opens a little more and Tika sees Jiri over Anna's shoulder and he looks as though he has come up from some horror—it catches Tika in her stomach and throat. His face is wet with tears, his chin struggles; the living room and dark balcony are behind him, and then he recognizes Tika and starts to smile. Tika says to Anna quietly, "Is Jiri okay, Anna?"

"He is having"—Anna waves her hand for the word, then gestures quickly for Tika to come in—"some emotions. From therapy today. But he is all right, honey. No worries. Thank you for the tomatoes. Come, come."

Clutching the plastic bowl of salad, Tika follows Anna's small back toward the kitchen: Jiri is gone from the living room and Tika assumes he has stepped onto the balcony. The kitchen smells strongly, wonderfully, of broiled meat and onion and garlic. Anna hefts the tomatoes onto the center island and motions to Tika to sit, but Tika is already doing so, at the chair that looks out over the garage roof and then back, between trees, to Irving Street. She sets her camera case on the table. Anna leaves the room a moment, and Tika hears her converse in Czech with Jiri, tones, on both sides, of reassurance. The window beside Tika is fully open to the screen. Tika thinks of Jiri's car in the garage, of how Jiri speaks of driving it again. It represents freedom to him, she knows; he said this once on a journey to the Arboretum, Tika driving Susan's clunky old Ford. *This is a gift for me, Tika,* Jiri said. *To drive with you. I'm worried about driving with Anna—she gets very nervous behind the wheel because she was always used to me driving. But you drive very well.*

Tika doesn't know if Jiri will be able to drive again—she has a feeling he will not—but she keeps encouraging him because you never know. His eye doctor at Massachusetts Eye and Ear says it is still a possibility. She's had it in mind to perhaps take Jiri to the mountains of New Hampshire for an afternoon, to see the early colors of fall. It would be safer for them to go in Jiri's Buick, and Jiri might enjoy that more. Jiri has said he's always loved mountains and has told her many stories about his excursions to the Alps of southern Bavaria after the war. Tika imagines her friend's face, happy, taking in the New Hampshire mountains, the orange and scarlet red of the trees.

But the image of his face moments ago comes back to her— what happened in the damn therapy? And *now* she remembers the rest of her nightmare, the red of the old curtains that looked somehow supernatural in the prefilm light. The theater was crowded, people settling in their seats. She had been very concerned for Jiri—where *was* he? And then she had seen him with the strange, dark man, accepting with considered sadness what the man had to say. She could not make her way to her friend through all of the bodies, people dipping and turning in her way, taking off coats, putting brochures on seats. Laughing (how *could* they be laughing, she'd thought in her dream; *how could they live their simple, everyday, luxurious lives with Jiri in trouble?*): She began to shout, angrily, *Don't listen to him, Jiri.* Tika had woken, crying, with Jesse holding her, saying, *Honey, honey. It's all right, honey.*

Now Anna bustles back into the kitchen, and Tika smiles bravely at her.

"So did you have the photography history today?"

Dr. Corliss had lowered the large blinds; the square of the television had blinked at the class. There had been the sounds of Tremont Street below the window. Tika nods. "We saw a film. On Matthew Brady."

"Ano," Anna says. "He was very important. He made"—she waves her wooden spoon—"a window for everyone, for the whole world—"

"Some of the Civil War stuff is so *sad,* when you look hard at it. All these *boys*—"

"Ano," Anna says, shaking her head. "The world has sometimes"—another wave of the spoon—"too many things, too much sadness."

She is speaking of her husband now, of course. Once in the hospital this June, when Jiri was sleeping, Anna had told Tika in the hallway that Jiri lost his family to the Nazis during the war, that they had killed the men and children of Lidice and sent the women to concentration camps. *They shot all the men,* Anna said. *Every male over fifteen. Jiri's father died there. They gassed the children in the back of a truck at Chelmno in Poland—eighty-two children, three of them were only one year old,* Anna said, *can you believe? Jiri narrowly escaped, but never found what had happened with his mother and sister.*

His sister? Tika had said.

She was just a little younger than you, Anna said.

He never found them? Tika had asked.

He looked for years, Anna said. *When he worked with U.S. intelligence, in Germany. Most of the women went to Ravensbrück. But Jana and Helena were never there.*

Why did the Nazis do it? Tika asked.

It was just insanity, Anna told her. *Hitler taking revenge for the Resistance killing of his general Heydrich. But no one in the village was involved. No one. Everyone in the village was innocent.*

Tika had gone home and looked up Lidice in the encyclopedia. There was a photograph of three Nazi soldiers, standing with odd smiles on their faces and with the town demolished and in rubble behind them. One of the Nazis had a boot set on a concrete girder, and looked as if he were simply at work on a construction site. Tika had felt her fingers cold on the pages of the book.

Anna, too, had lost her father in that war, in the uprising in Prague, in 1945. Tika imagines Jesse in combat, running by a barbed-wire fence at night, explosions lighting the sky behind him. It is the image that comes to her when she thinks of war. Barbarism, insanity—human bodies scattered like bloody dolls, as in today's film. She could never let her lover go into such a thing.

"I never spoke with Jiri about his town," Tika says quietly. "I didn't know if he wanted to be reminded of it. But it looked to me like he wanted to talk about something the other day, when we were at the Arboretum."

"I know," Anna says, whispering over the sound of the cooking. "He does not even speak to me much about it, even in fifty-two years of marriage. But he is remembering much more now, because of the therapy." She puts plates on the counter, and Tika gets up and takes them to the dining room. When Tika comes back into the kitchen Anna asks, a little more loudly, "So how is the project?"

"I did a lot of darkroom stuff today," Tika says. "I'm pretty far ahead on my photographs."

Anna nods. She stirs tomato paste, then begins adding paprika, thyme, rosemary, red and green peppers, and mushrooms into the mix. She shakes the pan expertly and stirs again. The pan sizzles anew. She says, "I like your photographs very much. When you brought them over. You have a real talent." She lowers her voice again. "I'll go back to the studio for a few hours tomorrow."

"I have time tomorrow in the afternoon, Anna," Tika says softly. "Do you want me to come stay with him?"

"*Nay*—" Anna waves her spoon. "I want him to be by himself for a while. I feel he needs this."

Tika watches Anna in her print dress, small blue and red flowers on a wild field, the apron about her, her glasses hanging on her chest. Since the first stroke, and especially since the brain hemorrhage in June, the old lady has lived on the tightrope with Jiri, trying to make sure his Coumadin doses strike the balance between dangers—too little of the drug and he might have a stroke again; too much and there might be bleeding on the brain again. Anna has had, constantly, to attend to his spirit—getting him out, conversing easily with him and hiding her worry, joking with him. Tika feels, looking at her, the months of struggle in the small, busy frame. She says: "I have to learn to cook like you, Anna."

"I learned from my mother," Anna says, adding beef stock, then Worcestershire sauce. "Markéta did not want to learn from me, so I shall teach you."

"It smells delicious."

"*Ano*. I shall teach you."

Tika nods. She gets up and takes herb croutons in a box from one of Anna's cabinets, and two wooden forks from a drawer. She brings her bowl of salad back to the table. She unwraps the plastic covering from the salad bowl, and opens the box and pours in the croutons and stirs them into the salad with the wooden forks. Anna

hands her vinaigrette sauce to work into the mix. The long rooftop
of the garage is dark now below Tika, leaves stretching over the
moss-covered shingles, and she can see the lights of Irving Street
blinking through the trees. She thinks of Professor Corliss speaking today about how, after the Civil War, thousands of Matthew
Brady's glass negatives were thought abandoned and used for
greenhouse windows, history slowly, over years, disintegrating in
the sun. Maybe that is like what is happening to Jiri.

When she looks up again Anna is nodding to her, saying quietly,
"I think he is better. You can go to him if you wish."

From the balcony doorway Tika sees the creases of Jiri's neck, the
side of his face in shadow. He sits very still with the old Grundig
radio on beside him. A broadcaster is talking about the intern in
Washington; she has been missing now for four months and the
congressman, Condit, is insisting that he had nothing to do with
her disappearance.

Tika thinks Jiri might be asleep, but he senses her there when
she has taken a few more steps and he turns and holds out a hand.
She slips into the rocker beside him and takes his hand and his
gray-blue eyes sparkle with charm. He clicks off the radio. He is a
handsome man; she has seen pictures of him in his late twenties,
when he worked in Germany: tweed coat and silk tie—devastating,
really. His face still has that easy confidence, and there is no hint
of the agony and confusion she saw there when she came in.

"So," Jiri says. "Is she nearly ready for us?"

"I think so," Tika says. "She says she will teach me to cook."

Jiri nods at this. "It is a good thing to know. A whole universe."

He pauses a moment, searching for words. "I never learned it, beyond a few bachelor, fast things. My mother and my sister were good cooks, but these things the men did not do as much in Czechoslovakia."

Tika holds Jiri's hand in both of her own. Closes her eyes. Breathes this connection. It is a hand with fine fingers and you can feel that it once had power. A large vein runs across the back of it to the smallest knuckle.

"You will see your boyfriend tonight?" Jiri says.

Tika opens her eyes. "He has a show in Central Square," she says.

"Well, I like him. But I am jealous."

"Jiri, you're *funny.*"

"You are working on the project?"

"Maybe I'll get a few shots. You're lucky if you get one or two out of a whole roll of film."

"How is it with the CD?" Jiri asks.

"They've almost finished it," Tika says. She told Jiri this the other day at the Arboretum, how the band is finishing up recording at a digital studio in Brookline, but he has forgotten. "I brought the first single to WECR and some other college stations last week, and it is already getting a lot of rotation."

"Rotation?"

"They're getting a lot of requests for it. Since they've been on the radio they're already recognized a lot more. Tonight's in this kind of funky place a few blocks off Mass Ave. I think they'll have a pretty good crowd there."

"You have to watch yourself around these places. The alleys around them are not always so safe. You have to stay around the boys."

"Jiri, I *know*. You don't have to worry about me."

"They're talking about this girl, this intern. It is a very dangerous world."

"People are saying the congressman had somebody do it," Tika says.

"I wouldn't doubt it," Jiri says. "There are people walking around who would tear down the sun if it would serve them."

"I'll be all right, Jiri," Tika says. "No worries. In these things I'm always with Jesse."

"Well, he's a good kid," Jiri says.

"Mohu Vás pozvat na večeři?" Anna is calling, from the dining room.

"That is my other girlfriend," Jiri says. "She is asking if she can invite us to dinner."

The dining room is small and formal and simple. Two windows look through leaves onto Trowbridge Street. A mahogany table with long-backed chairs stands on a deep Oriental rug, and there are no paintings on the cream-colored walls; the large chandelier over the dining table is dimmed and Anna has lit slender white candles. Tika walks with Jiri slowly, her hand on his arm, until he slides her chair out for her and seats her, and he stands at his place until Anna has everything on the table, plates of fettuccine topped with sauced steak and peppers and with Tika's salad to the side (Tika notices that the Posselts never put salad in a separate dish) and wine. Tika reads the label—an Italian red—and she imagines her father walking with her in Rome, when she was thirteen, his face turning to smile at her, gentle and happy, the sky pink behind him.

Then they are all eating, and Tika has to check herself, the dinner is so good, and remind herself not to eat the way she does in the Emerson Café, so fast.

"*Z čeho je to?*" Jiri says.

"With arrowroot," Anna says.

"It's good," Jiri says, his eyebrows up. And then to Tika: "I'm asking how she makes the sauce."

Since the strokes, Anna has been trying to cut down on the fat content of their meals. Sometimes, when Tika comes over, Anna is making fastidious notes from low-fat cookbooks she has taken from the library.

"It's great, Anna," Tika says. "Amazing that it's *healthy*, too."

"We must have Jesse to dinner soon again," Jiri says.

"He would like that," Tika says, looking down. "He really likes you guys." For a moment, she feels she might weep at the parental gesture. Her mind is filled with many things: The woman in Australia is brushing hair away from her forehead, and there is the sound of a television from the next room. In New Hampshire Susan's feet are curled around the back of the husband; Stuart Livesy's descending shoulders are valleys and shadows of light. She hears Susan's voice saying, *He fucks like a rabbit.*

"Tika?" Anna says. "You don't seem entirely yourself. Are you all right?"

"I'm sorry," Tika says, watching the old woman. She pauses. "It's Susan. She's seeing this married man. From Australia. I met him last night. At the apartment."

There is silence a moment from her hosts. Outside a series of cars goes by on Kirkland, wheels whispering. The protective bird is sounding its repeating, whistling pattern, rising and dropping again.

"That's a problem," Anna says, as Jiri breathes out heavily. "Nothing good comes from these kinds of things, from lying."

"That's what bothers me. I'm part of the lie," Tika says.

In the kitchen last night, Susan kissed Stuart's hand: an expensive Rolex watch there on that wrist, a present, perhaps, from the wife. Tika had tried to strike a nonchalant pose, to smile and converse easily with her roommate's new lover in a way that didn't show her judgment, her concern. She knows that she didn't pull it off. She has met, since last winter when she moved in with Susan, four of Susan's lovers, some of whom Susan was seeing simultaneously. That was Susan's business. But Stuart Livesy is married, and there a wife in Australia, and this is in Tika's home now.

"And your feelings about your friend have changed," Jiri says.

"Yes," Tika says. "I feel badly about that, too. I'm mad I didn't say anything when they were planning it because I knew I would feel this way, and I didn't listen to myself."

"Susan is thinking only of herself in this," Anna says, her voice lowered again, as if the three of them are joined in conspiracy. "Maybe she thinks she can't help it. But she should have thought of how bringing him home would affect you. Perhaps she did. Perhaps she wanted to feel less guilty herself and bringing you into it makes it less of a personal burden."

Jiri, his face set firmly, looks at his wife, weighing this pronouncement of hers with concern. It is dark outside now. Tika feels as if somehow she is rising above herself, rising to look down on this discussion, something rushing in her ears. The candles throw their shadows onto the walls, and the great protective shapes of Anna and Jiri hover over her own image in the deepening hues of night.

THREE

Below on Trowbridge Street, Ghost-Man looks up and sees the quarter moon shining brightly through leaves and a black explosion of clouds. The run of old brownstones, of dark gardens and blue-lit windows, is alive with sounds you will never hear in winter: dishes being put away after dinners, female voices reestablishing the normalcy of their households with gossip, insects, dogs barking, televisions playing sports and evening detective shows. The greater commotion that was here at the end of the afternoon, when Ghost-Man made a brief pass through in his car—the early evening business when Trowbridge Street was a bottleneck of other cars and pedestrians returning from the day—is completely gone now. The street itself is a tunnel, punctuated by circles from streetlamps, waiting for him.

He hears a cat yowl in the next neighborhood over, on Irving, and a truck rumbles somewhere in the vicinity of Kirkland, where Ghost-Man parked his Mazda. Somewhere, now, there are the shouts of children. These sounds seem so close it is as if they are

those of other ghosts on this quiet thoroughfare, amplified in the
night like the simmering, last quarter moon.

Ghost-Man starts walking very quickly and methodically and
with a package held tight to his body. It is a ten-by-thirteen-inch
mailer tied with twine and addressed to him from the *Williams,
Iannucci, Traupman and Hoyt* law firm of Portland, Maine, and the
cardboard edges of it are worn from the working of his hand. He
steps over the sidewalk as if he quite certainly has somewhere to
go. Past this house painted slate blue, number 18, with the white
balcony fence that has ivy crawling over it; by this beech tree
where the sidewalk is cracked. Many times, standing by this tree as
if waiting for a ride, he has glanced in at Monica Wood in 18A doing her yoga. He has watched her shadowed figure, slightly overweight, her arms arched above her, her brown ponytail dipping as
she goes from side to side, disappearing, then coming up again as
the female voice says, *Up, and now all the way down and to the side,*
and when Ghost-Man feels the plausibility of his presence exhausted he will quickly step away, his insides singing with that
curve of flesh, the outstretched hand through underside of arm to
hip, his heart wanting to stay, to fly into that window.

Monica Wood's apartment is dark now; she is not home. Her
place is one of crowded furniture and many cookbooks and in-
cense candles. She has consistently vacuumed rugs and a wall in
the kitchen laden with Post-it memos that will sometimes stay
there for two weeks before being crumpled and tossed into the
white designer pail. When she is gone he will slip her lock with a
credit card and read the mail that she leaves opened by the refrigerator (gourmet and yoga and gossip magazines, myriad bills from
banks). Once, very late at night, he came in and she was asleep and
he sat on her corduroy-covered living room couch; he'd closed his

eyes in that darkness and listened to the breathing of the woman in her bedroom, thrilling at his proximity to her, at what she didn't know.

He has imagined, in his nights, Monica Wood and her flesh and woman-smell beside him. But hers is one of the many female homes he visits here on Trowbridge Street, and it is never wise to become fixed on any one woman. In other neighborhoods, at other times, his fixations have led to a loss of control, and he has had some narrow escapes. One must always abandon specific desire to survive as a man, and one must always have another story to go to. This is true for all men, all the world over, Ghost-Man knows.

A burst of traffic hisses by behind him on Kirkland, and he thinks of the long parade of men, the long parade of hopeful sperm, making up their stories, their lies, just to be in the vicinity of the egg. And what happens to those men who don't get an egg? His shadow scallops beneath a streetlight, blends with dark tar again, that quick, purposeful silhouette with the package beneath the arm.

The cicadas are quite loud in the hedges by 24, and there he stops, for a light is on in the second-floor apartment and the shadow of an elm tree and a streetlight that is out give him ample cover. There Dr. Heather Stolz is reading a book, her head bowed in great concentration. The arc lamp above her couch illuminates her hair; her face is dark. Eight years ago, she published an award-winning thesis on gravity modification; she is thirty-four years old and teaches physics at Harvard. Her Ph.D. is from Rensselaer and she has done work for NASA's Marshall Space Flight Center. Her book is still available on Amazon.com, but Ghost-Man has not ordered it. He has never seen her close up; from the pictures in her apartment and on her book in the Amazon.com ad she appears pretty, with small features and brown eyes. She is a runner, and in her mail are always magazines and other literature devoted to the sport. She keeps a neat place, and has something of a fetish about oiling her wooden furniture. She has a cat that tilts its ears back and growls and goes under the couch when Ghost-Man comes through the door. Her apartment is the only one on that hallway, a landing, really, and the stairs to her place are mercifully covered in deep brown carpet. He has watched her comb her hair in the bathroom at night (the bathroom, if illuminated, would be just there to the right); he has imagined being within her, in her bed, her head whipping into the pillow in a frenzy.

He looks up at the fall of hair over her brow. He is still in the elm-deepened shadow, but he feels, for a moment, danger here; his is a face with high cheekbones and thinning hair that is swept back tightly to his skull. He is dressed as if having just left a job with a casual dress code: neat black pants, loafers, a blue short-sleeved cotton shirt. He has powerful, large hands, and the right one works on the package tightly. Then the hand is still, as he senses something; someone has glanced out their window as they've come into a TV room, before turning on a light, and they have seen a man alone on a sidewalk, looking up at an apartment. Silly to ignore this smell in the air, this thing that could make him prey! He begins, with some deliberation, to walk again. The physics teacher dissolves in him; her flesh becomes this street, this danger that has just whispered by him like a breath of wind. He hopes it was a man looking out whichever of these hundreds of windows the look came from. A man would glance and shrug and turn on lights and the *Monday Night Football* game. But women are highly developed in sensing things. You can fool them about your personality, for a time, your intentions, because so many of them want to believe first in the human heart, but about things like this—a displaced soul in the world—women have an *instinct*, women are *sharp*. They can see things a man never will. Ghost-Man has fought in combat with men; he remembers sand on streets, sand everywhere, bright sun, the controlled kick of his M-16 at the press of trigger, *chit chit chit*. An Iraqi man still in motion before him, dead as he fell, a loop of red behind in the dusty road. The Iraqi still moving a moment in the sand, then the quiet of that white street. It is easy, fighting with men: You are killed or you kill. Men are just brutal, just straight on, but women *feel* things, they fucking *analyze*. You get over here, in Cambridge, where the women are always busy, it seems, with self-improvement, doing their meditation in candlelit rooms (Ghost-Man has watched a number of such demonstrations back in 18A—he has seen, from the sumac-protected rise at the side of the building, Monica Wood and five other women gather on Wednesday nights, sitting cross-legged on the floor, candles burning in the center of their circle), and unless you engage them romantically (you can lead a woman literally anywhere then), you are *always* suspect, especially with the older ones, aged forty, fifty, who have had their share of hard knocks for believing too fervently in the male heart.

Two poodles bark at him from the windows of 26, startling him. Their tiny eyes stare furiously out at his movement; their paws scratch the glass. He crosses the street quickly, threading between a Saab and a Volvo, to 37. He feels the sweat of his hands on the cardboard. Those fucking things just about made him jump out of his skin. If Ghost-Man needs an escape he can follow the walkways here back into the weeds, sliding behind the garages of the two buildings (they are nearly joined) and a high stand of grass and sumacs and one more, broken shed and then a dash for a break in the fence leading to Irving; a quick right onto Irving Terrace, which spills out onto Summer Street, and he can walk the streets calmly to his car. But no one comes out a door to see what the dogs were barking at.

It is extremely dark on this sidewalk, for another streetlight above is out, and a zelkova tree over Ghost-Man is a solid ceiling of leaves. He stops before a garden, sunflowers brushing the lower sill of a window. He breathes, hears his expectant heart hammering. The garden belongs to a fortyish painter named Alison Tiner who lives on this lower floor; she is apparently quite famous. Her living room is a studio—her paintings are pretty wild stuff: vibrant, dark stretches of canvas. Sometimes Ghost-Man sits in the middle of her floor, looking at these creations, these fragments of Alison Tiner: A female figure—Alison—masturbates on a bed, her head turned away on the pillow; in her doorway is a silhouette of a man with a cocked fist. In another painting a standing, naked man and three women, one of whom is Alison, their hands all joined, lean back their heads in some bedroom darkness as if howling, and you can see white horseshoes of their teeth, their white eyes looking up in anguish.

The painter draws her curtains over opened windows at night, but when her lights are on Ghost-Man can see her form, and some nights, during the last two months that he has been occupying the Trowbridge Street neighborhood, another form there has been that of a man, both of these often extraordinarily exaggerated by their proximity to a low-lying lamp. Tonight at first he sees nothing, and then the shadow of Alison Tiner suddenly walks across the slow-moving curtains. He steps back a little into shadows. The woman's strange silhouette head is nodding into the phone, her hand holding the phone cord.

"Wait a minute honey, let me get a pen," she says.

Isn't that funny? That lightness in her voice? It isn't there when she talks to her family from the West Coast—those conversations are usually conducted in a monotone or at best with very slight enthusiasm—but here, in this shadow play across the window, her voice is staged. And of course it is so, for she is auditioning; that is how it goes, always, a woman auditions, a man judges how comfortable he is with the woman, but he never gets the real story. If the woman passes the audition and draws him in with her sex, he will think then that he is in love, and she will run the *universe,* he will walk and *breathe* according to her agenda. He will go to work and break his back on the wheel of commerce, but he will never really be successful enough to prove that he is worthy. He will revolve with all other men around that bright, miraculous sun, that blinding light. *She* and *she* and *she* and *she,* there on a sunny day, your beautiful wife talking with neighbors on the sidewalk, mothers joggling their infant strollers; light filters down through leaves onto her face. She walks in town, runs into a man who is handsome, tall, with old wealth; she shades her eyes with a hand to see him. She pushes his shoulder in jest at something said, something suggested. And when the woman envelops that other flesh, you lose your sun, you lose your *life,* because she can say any damn thing about you to clear you away from her like debris, like detritus; it is amazing how swiftly a woman can do this. You break off from your orbit and spin into space, wildly. It drives you to your knees, woman-loss, end of woman agenda. Ghost-Man knows all about it.

"Okay, I'm back, sweetie," Alison Tiner says. She is leaning down now, and Ghost-Man can see her form lurching a moment across the curtains. "Flight 202C coming in from Atlanta. Two-

seventeen . . . No, honey, it's fine. It's not like I have to get anywhere in the morning. I'll even whip us up something to eat when
we get in tonight."

Ghost-Man breathes the scent of the sunflowers in the darkness. They are nodding toward the window, whispering. *She* and
she and *she* and *she*. Down the street a dog, a shepherd, goes into a
fit of deep barking—the dog is to the right there, in the brownstone
at 26. Dogs are like women, this extraordinary instinct that something is very wrong.

"Good, honey. I can't wait to see you, too." Alison Tiner's
shadow hangs up the phone. The dog barks again suddenly, franti-
cally. *You are right, dog,* Ghost-Man thinks, *but I'm afraid you're giving me away.* There is a female voice of admonishment, and the
barking stops, and another angry male voice rises, and then all is
quiet: The dog has been put out on a line. And then Ghost-Man
can hear all of the things the dog does, as if he has the ears of that
canine: hears cutlery in that house snapping and clashing, a reaction to the emotion of the shepherd, to the emotion within that
place; something is not right with that young couple (their name is
Meacham—they moved in just one month ago, the wife precisely
directing the husband and his friends as they bumped with all the
furniture into the building. Valerie Meacham has many versions of
sleeping pills and relaxants in her medicine cabinet, Halcion, Val-
ium, Xanax). Ghost-Man hears metal runners as the dog goes, back
and forth, on his line, this harsh sound of frustration. Later, the
shepherd will be banished to his clean, shining-metal doghouse,
but his ears, his senses, will be quick to alert.

Above, there is the language like the Russian Ghost-Man heard
sometimes in the Mideast, but with more of a hushing quality to it;
he ducks a little into the shadows and looks up, but the window of

the old European couple is at too steep an angle for him to be noticed. The voice of an American woman says, "I'll get that, Anna," over running water. This is Tika LaFond, who dines there often: Ghost-Man closes his eyes in this sunflower darkness, breathes deeply, imagines the scent of Tika's white cotton coverlet, the fragrance of skin lotion there, just after she has showered and gone out. He was there this evening when she was showering, pressed to the wall just beneath the bathroom window, listening to that water, how her body altered the velocity of the spray. He was there earlier this morning. Sunflowers before him grow; he hears a steady crackle of stems and capitula, thousands of eyes stare from endless circles of orange black. Alison Tiner is bending, writing something.

He can sense the rush of fire: this from the street performers blocks away in Harvard Square who, with a gaggle of people around them, take torches and dip them into raised mouths, so that the flame is burning within their throats (Ghost-Man imagines fire smoldering within human red, tunnels of wet flesh), then removed, swaths of orange blue heat against the night. Alison Tiner is gone from the window now; later, he shall find out what sort of evening she has in mind for her gentleman. But first there is something that he must do.

In twenty minutes Ghost-Man is behind 38; there is a spread of elm trees here, a strong smell of earth and the cement of the garages. On Monday nights Tika LaFond and Susan Bristol are often gone until midnight or one o'clock. Ghost-Man watched Tika LaFond come down the steps of 39 ten minutes ago and wave to the old man on the balcony above. The man spoke to her in that language, and she laughed and waved and said, Don't worry, Jiri, I'll be fine. She was carrying her camera case and she turned onto Cambridge Avenue, toward Harvard Square. She is going to her job at the pub or to see her musician (hard to tell, for she carries the camera case with her always); Susan Bristol left with the Australian man earlier—Ghost-Man saw them packing when he came through Trowbridge in his car—the Australian putting a suitcase into the back of Susan Bristol's Ford.

The women leave the back door, where there is a wonderful blackness, simply open. Tika LaFond with her new, short-cut hair makes Ghost-Man think, as he goes quickly up the wooden steps, of the Admiral, the club he will be at later in Medford. There is a dancer there named Velvet Queen, who has short-cut black hair and violet eyes and black vinyl boots—a slender, then wide back like Tika's and a proud neck and long, long legs; Velvet Queen comes to the stage completely swathed in darkness, in dark veils that swirl about her. Last night, the dancer was sitting to the side of the entrance and recognized Ghost-Man as he came in. She motioned him over, and when he bought her a drink she was unusually talkative; she told him about the massage therapy she was learning, the money she was putting away for a house. She caught him looking at her with his yearning and smiled, and stretched there, with her elbows back on the bar, ran a hand through her hair, let him wish. He likes to see Velvet Queen talk, likes to watch her face, so bold and perfect and frightening in its makeup. He enjoys that she can take him into her confidence so easily and then quickly slip into being a slightly cruel woman. She whispers words into his ear, asks him which of the dancers he likes—Shiloh, on the main stage? Tanya or Autumn in the circles? *You,* Ghost-Man says. *Good answer,* Velvet Queen will say, smiling with her bloodred lips.

Tika LaFond has a different color of hair, a more golden hue of skin, but she moves in a similar way as the dancer, and sometimes, late at night, Ghost-Man stands on the porch in front of this building where, if you look carefully and patiently through the thin lace curtains, you can watch the girl sleeping, make out the way her mouth parts as she dreams. She is like Velvet Queen before corruption, before poor decisions set her into the sexual fishbowl, the circle of wishing men.

He takes very light cotton gloves from his pocket and puts them on. Into that back door: It is easy on its hinges, making no noise, staying finally, as always, a few centimeters open. He trembles, flushed with adrenaline and fear. Ghost-Man takes off one glove and reaches into a shirt pocket for methamphetamine, his second pill of the night. He puts it on his tongue, swallows, puts the glove back on. He can hardly wait for the soaring, the rush in his legs and chest that makes him feel as if he is watching Velvet Queen onstage, when the dancer locks her high-heeled boots on either side of him and moves her body at him. It is so fucking dark in here, and he cannot make mistakes, so he waits, lets his eyes adjust so he doesn't knock some damn thing over; Ghost-Man has an image of Susan Bristol for a moment, with her chin jutting out, walking out of this house to the back garage, to her old Ford, on a day of rain. This was in July, his first month of Trowbridge occupation. She had been talking to herself, and it was very matter-of-fact, direct talk, as if she were trying to reason something out with someone. Standing in a shadow at the back fence of the Topalka house, Ghost-Man had been unable to make out what the girl was saying, but she slammed the Ford's door harder than she usually did and fairly rocketed backward out of the cement garage.

Now he sees a glimmer of Susan Bristol's bike, the rattling old Schwinn with its basket, and he moves to it and closes his eyes

(there is not much to see in here, anyway, beyond the outlines of
the school through a dusty glass window) and imagines that he can
smell Susan Bristol's chamomile shampoo, the nice bite of it; he
runs his fingers over the handlebars of the bike and hears them
slide there, dry, and feels the girl's restlessness. His fingers go over
the seat, sensing the split of woman. He smells mildew in this
wooden, close darkness, and when he opens his eyes he is facing
the door and the slight vertical line of light, and about eye level,
working its way down the length of door, a large centipede is filing
its legs steadily, the head occasionally stopping, probing, a hateful
motion against the night. Ghost-Man is startled, then angry, to
open his eyes upon this. He takes an old newspaper from the plastic recycling box, rolls it up, tips the door out, and brushes the large
insect toward the outdoors, then replaces the newspaper quickly,
just in case the centipede managed to somehow cling to the paper.
He hates those fucking things.

   He steps quickly into the apartment—to civilization. There is
still the smell of Tika LaFond in the air—of her coconut shampoo.
Tika is the more attractive of the girls, but the brunette Susan often dries herself after she showers in the kitchen window, where
she believes no one will see her; only the Topalka wall is there, the
garden, the sunflowers, without a window. Susan's breasts are naturally, beautifully large and tug with her drying. Ghost-Man once
smiled, one summer evening, hearing Tika LaFond admonish her
roommate for being naked before the glass. Susan had said, *We live
in the* city. *Creeps are everywhere. I'll live the way I want to live.* It's
the only time Ghost-Man has heard them fight, though when he
sees sneakers that have been thrown against the wall in Susan Bristol's room or a coat or hairbrush tossed in haste on Tika LaFond's
bed he can tell that the females have been quietly angry with each

other. The hairbrush was on Tika LaFond's bed this morning; her bed, too, was unmade, truly uncharacteristic of her.

Susan Bristol is usually mixing the towel drying with eating something from the refrigerator, and now, stepping into the kitchen, Ghost-Man hears the refrigerator come on, as if on cue. He does not open it for fear of any sudden, unexplainable crack of light in this place, and that makes him think again of the centipede filing, filing downward, and he thinks if somehow he found a centipede on the refrigerator door it would be so maddening and frightening that he would have to leave quickly.

But there is a homey smell to this place where the girls cook; one of them—he assumes it was Susan Bristol—has made spaghetti this night, and Ghost-Man smells thyme, basil, garlic. He takes the K-Bar knife from his packet (he has wiped it only in leaves), draws it from its sheath, and turns on the faucet. He washes the knife, letting the hot water run over the blade; the sink is dark, the water a black, refracted flow off the steel. It is dangerous to leave the water on for too long: He shuts off the faucet and swings the knife over the drain, air-drying it, then tugs his shirt out of his pants and dries the metal thoroughly, and returns the knife to its sheath, and the sheath back to the package. The package is tight now with the papers and the knife. He tucks in his dampened shirttail.

Light stretches in from the windows facing the street; the floorboards have a creak to them, so Ghost-Man steps across them in a pattern that has proved quiet in the past, and then he is on the rug, and he crosses the living room to the darker hallway. The phone message counter there reads 0, glowing on the small mahogany table. There is mail for Susan by the phone. He picks up the envelopes carefully and reads them, replaces them. He glances into

Susan Bristol's room: dark swatches of lace over her windows in sweeping, upturned V's (in daylight the material is violet) and the hideous chair—straight, high-backed, gothic swirls of wood—in a corner by the wide bed. The chair makes him shudder; it might have been reserved for a judge in Salem three hundred years ago. It is Susan Bristol's chair because the Ford is Susan Bristol's car, because the blunt clogs she wears are her shoes; she loves boxy things that suggest a certain masculinity, a certain territory she has a right to. There is a framed portrait of Marilyn Monroe over the bed, a faint, enticing set of curved lines in these shadows.

It is much easier to see in Tika LaFond's room, for here the streetlights send triangles of pale light across the floor, the Lennon drawing, the mirror. Only the numerous books on photography, set in shelves against the northern wall, are in complete darkness. The bed is made now. Ghost-Man kneels and puts his package on edge against a leg of the bed and lowers his face and smells the cotton coverlet, the girl there: soap like lemons, legs smoothed with lotion, the apricot scent of the gel she uses in her hair. He buries his nose and breathes, surrenders to it, makes a noise in his throat. There is so much that he would like to tell this girl, that he *must* tell this girl. He slips his hand beneath the bed, finds the shoebox, takes it out, and places it on the coverlet. There are two cards from the famous sister since he last checked: birds lighting on a fountain in Milan; Carnival in Rio. He turns and stands and looks and, just below the mirror, there is a new postcard of Christ above the city, His arms spread—beyond Him city, sea, a fading horizon like something from a fairy-tale. Ghost-Man had his honeymoon in Rio, during Carnival; he remembers the brightness, the quick, glad eyes of women, his own wife, Jenna, looking very white next to all of those dark skins.

He picks up the card and tilts it over to read Kascha's message.

He puts it back at the same angle on the dresser, on top of the bills. There is a small photograph of the sister on the opposite wall: a face nearly that of Tika's—Ghost-Man has seen Kascha LaFond in advertisements for beer and whiskey, in glass city windows advertising perfume, jeans, Internet sites, and even on the huge billboard above the Admiral, selling gin. When he sees the famous eyes looking at him, Ghost-Man senses that he shares a secret with the model about her younger sibling. *We know, don't we, what a woman can do to a man, but Tika still does not know.* He turns and puts the two postcards back in the box in order, and slips the box in place under the bed.

He thinks of Tika sleeping here, on her back, idly stretching her legs. Here, right here: He is in the universe of her. He gets up and takes two steps and opens the closet. He parts dresses, some in plastic bags, and he can smell the plastic and Tika LaFond's lavender perfume, and he turns around and pushes into that darkness backward, the shutterlike doors swinging slightly shut behind him. He can rest here, against plastic and cloth; he smells the darkness, the fragrance of these dresses, these skins of the girl. Sheath and georgette chemise dresses and short-sleeved sweaters and skirts of cotton and rayon; he is closest to a smooth black skimmer dress that she wore recently to a party with her boyfriend. He remembers now how, from the shadows of the willows across the street, he'd watched her get out of the boyfriend's van when they returned, wearing high-heeled sandals and this dress that flowed so beautifully about her legs. Her dark-haired musician talking, joking a little with her, Tika LaFond smiling up at him. Then on the porch teasing her musician, holding his collar, saying, *Just come inside and fuck me,* uncharacteristic of her, really, something like her slut roommate Susan would do.

Ghost-Man brushes the dress with his forearm and hand, moves it against his cheek. And he is a boy in Kentucky, at the condominium complex that is over the hill from his mother's home; he plays with some boys there and one boy named Jim Dorling has a very beautiful mother who wears dresses like this and takes off her high heels and sinks into the couch when she returns home from work, with her legs tucked under her and a drink, and she talks to the boys kindly and as if they are adults and asks them about their day at school. The woman has black hair cut short and wide, beautiful eyes that take you seriously when you talk to her. Then Ghost-Man is on school grounds, just a short walk from his home. It is recess and the teachers are calling the children in from the swing sets and the children are already lining up at the brick stairs but he does not go in. He begins to climb the chain of one of the swings, as high as he can, and Mrs. Dorling is one of the recess monitors today, calling him, and he is rubbing against the metal and cannot answer, can hardly move; other students, lined up at the door, are staring at him, small, writhing *him,* there on the tight metal, and Mrs. Dorling has come close and is looking up with her hand shading her eyes and saying, *It's okay, honey, just come on down now,* and he slides down, still with that unbearable soaring dance within him.

Here in the closet he grasps himself, remembering how the pain of his small shoulders, his body and the humiliation it caused, meant nothing next to that soaring. Squeezing through his trousers, surrounded by the skins of this other, regal girl. There is a honk of a car horn in the street, very close, that brings him back to reality.

Fool! What is he doing? He takes his hand roughly away from his erection and extracts himself from the closet, a brisk rustling of plastic and cloth; a moment later and he might have suffocated in his own weakness, might have lost his head enough to be discovered. He straightens out the plastic, the dresses and shirts, as best he can. The thought of Mrs. Dorling, of her eyes taking him so seriously, shames him, and he feels the blood in his face. He smoothes the bedspread and collects his cardboard container and checks the room quickly that nothing is out of place.

Very soon, he is outside again in the open darkness, slipping south, taking off the gloves and putting them in his pocket, going through the opening of the chain-link fence and onto the Trowbridge Academy lawn and emerging at Cambridge Avenue. He walks purposefully on the sidewalk. It is not hard to recover your equilibrium here, with cars passing by and shops lit brightly, an anonymous, innocent brightness, the package swinging quickly, like a pendulum, beneath your arm.

FOUR

Heart, to whom will you cry? *Wem willst du klagen, Herz?*
Rainer Maria Rilke is here, in darkness on the library
wall: Jiri can recite the poem from his childhood. He can touch
these volumes even without light in the room; can name them in
order as he paces like a captain on a quarterdeck.

Remarque, Richter, Rilke, Rumi.

Salter, Seferis, Seifert, Shirer, Sis.

Škvorecky, Steinbeck, Sterling.

So how can he remember all of this, but not when he saw Tika
last? She was concerned about the adultery—the selfish damn Susan Bristol and the Australian—but whether it was this evening or
yesterday, or earlier in the week—this he cannot get a fix on. He
walks, leaning on his cane, trying to think it through. It must have
been tonight, sometime, for there are tomatoes in the kitchen, in a
bag, and those had to have been brought by Tika; he and Anna
have not had Vivian Topalka over for at least a week.

He makes hardly any noise in his slippers, on this carpeted
floor: Anna sleeps soundly in the next room. Here on a shelf, a

square in the darkness, is a photograph of his mother and sister that he took just a few days before the Nazis came. He'd left the spool of film in his coat pocket—the same coat he'd worn during his frantic escape. Though the photograph is indistinguishable, he pictures it precisely: his mother with her arm around his sister, his sister's hand on the seat of her bike. In the cool summer morning outside their home Helena is bemused, and his mother is laughing a little after hurrying Jiri to take the picture—*Jiri, your sister will be late for work! For heaven's sake, hurry it up!* Helena climbed on the bike afterward and pushed away from the curb, and her feet gained purchase with the pedals; she waved as she turned off Andělu, down Nova Street, and her hair and sweater blew behind her. Jiri remembers this, and his last moments with Helena, a few nights later—Helena asleep in her room, in the darkness, a triangle of moonlight above her head—before he went to the Krušina farm.

Then, after the long run to Plzeň, at the safe house of Dr. Jaroslav Kobera and Kobera's lover, Božena Krásová—the address his father sent him to—he knelt, wept beside a radio in Dr. Kobera's kitchen as Radio Berlin announced, matter-of-factly, the annihilation of his family. *All men of Lidice have been shot,* the announcer said. *The women deported to a concentration camp. The name of the village immediately abolished.* Later, in Germany, Jiri would see the precise 16 mm film the Nazis made, documenting the murder of his home. Every Lidice building wired with plastic explosives and blown to pieces. The church falling like sand. The graveyard bulldozed. German engineers had even diverted the stream to change the landscape.

And his father's body among the heap of others, at the Horák farm, where the men had been shot in groups of ten.

There in Dr. Kobera and Božena Krásová's kitchen, floorboards had rushed at Jiri: He'd dropped to his knees. An uncontrollable keening came from his chest and throat, and then the hands of Dr. Kobera and Božena were firmly on his shoulders; Božena Krásová spoke words into one of his ears, as if trying to keep him connected to life, to the oxygen above these waves.

Dr. Kobera and Božena ran the largest Resistance group in Bohemia, and Jiri found out that his uncle, Petr Jaroš, from Plzeň, belonged to it as well. For four years Jiri blew up ammunition depots, derailed trains, pulled Jews off the trains going to Terezín, and cut phone lines, thinking each day about the afternoon when, exhausted from his run, he'd found out about his family on Dr. Kobera's radio. His personality, his life, was severed in that moment and became something else. From then until the end of the war, he lived to avenge his family.

Jiri paces through the darkness, thinking of all of it, moving through history and memory and literature. His shadow on the wall goes back and forth. Winston Churchill is warning the world about the Nazi threat, and Rikki-Tikki-Tavi disappears into Nagaina's lair, sinking his teeth into her tail. Jack London's wolves move closer and closer to Henry's fire, even as the desperate, tired man thrusts burning wood at them. Picasso weeps for Guernica—a tumble of abstract, tortured spirits, of explosion and death. A Nazi officer, looking at the gigantic canvas with awe, asks the artist, *Did you do this?*

No, Picasso says. *You did.*

The white spider hovers, but is not, as before, coming out at Jiri. He stops and looks at it. There within that slip of spine Adolf

Hitler is seventeen, on the Promenade in Linz, with his friend August Kubíček, watching a beautiful young local girl named Stefanie; she has captured his attention so fiercely that the young Hitler can hardly live. She walks with her mother and occasionally a military officer will step up to her and offer a flower. *C'mon, Adolf,* Kubíček says. *Go and buy a rose and present it and tip your hat! Make your intentions known!* But Hitler shakes his head; he tells his friend, *Nein, esist nicht möglich. She would only laugh.* He has nothing to show for himself, no accomplishments. Still, the dark teenager has followed his Stefanie everywhere, has even dreamed of kidnapping her, of possessing her that way. Jiri imagines the psychotic, anguished boy in that fall of 1906; climbing the Freinberg late at night, overlooking Linz, the Danube a dark mirror below him. Making plans. *To be Wagner's Rienzi, to save my people.* Vast crowds will salute him with a massive *Heil!*

No Stefanie, no young woman, would dare ignore young Hitler's affections then.

Jiri paces away from the swastika, back to Rilke, back to his own childhood in Lidice. It is 1940. The light is bright on the walls of his schoolroom. He sits in his row, entranced by the words of the poem, listening to Professor Vošahlík read from the book:

> Früher. Klagtest. Was war? Eine gefallene
> Beere des Jubels, unreife.

"The poet is an older man now," says Professor Vošahlík, tapping fingers for emphasis on his desk, his other hand cradling the book.

The professor's prodigious eyebrows raise to emphasize his point. *"On cítí lítost víc než v minulsti.* He is feeling a sorrow greater than he has felt before."

The Lidice children, in their rows, listen attentively; the windows are large and the sunlight warms Jiri's shoulder. A girl smiles at Jiri—her face, sixty-one years ago, comes to him now clearly: green eyes, freckles, a sweep of dark chestnut hair, so that he stops in the darkness, smiling at the memory. It is as if she is in front of him. The class ends, dust swirling in a shaft of window light; the girl asks him to write his name in her leather pen case. Says she hears he is very good at the soccer. Her name is Marie Příhodová; she plays soccer, too. Later, Jiri walks with her on the cobblestones before St. Martin's Church, and they balance up on the Lidice walls, showing off.

Then it is a summer evening in 1942, and Jiri and Marie hold hands there, by the old wall, hearing above the swaying branches of trees. There are no lights on in their town, just all of these steep shapes and the sound of the evening wind. They are near the stream and they can hear the water, and beyond them are more walls of Lidice, houses with roofs of red shale, and the earth is turning and night is coming. Fanta pond sparkles dark painter's blue and silver beneath the stars. There, a few roofs up the hill, on Andělu, is the steep pitched roof of Jiri's house, the shape of the large oak tree, the plum trees behind. There is the scent of Bohemian night: stone and mortar and the wetness of the earth, a heavy fragrance of greenery, white willows and oaks here by the stream. It is a wonder, Marie's cheek now so close, her profile nearly touching Jiri's as they talk. Her voice in his ear. Her eyes shining when she brings her head back, to look at him.

But now my Tree of Joy is breaking, Professor Vošahlík reads,

What is breaking in the storm is my slowly
grown Tree of Joy.
The most beautiful thing in my invisible
landscape, which let me be seen
by the invisible angels.

Marie watches him. And here is Helena: Jiri, three years old,
leans out from behind the sunflower stalks where he has been hiding in the garden, and his sister's eyes are on him, full of play, and
she is saying, *Kam jdeš, Jirko? Where are you going? You can't escape
me.* Their mother calls them to dinner, and Jiri can hear his father's
voice in the house. There are crickets in the night.

In the darkness, here, the photograph of his mother and sister
stares out at Jiri, a fathomless hole.

During the brain hemorrhage last June Jiri had seen the walls of
Lidice on fire, and he was looking around for Helena. He was
shouting, terrified. *There were only the black walls on fire: no
houses, no people left.* He could not remember where he was. He
could remember Anna's name, for she was there, suddenly,
alarmed, leaning over him, but he was not sure if he was in Massachusetts or Seattle, or perhaps Prague; here was the painting of
John Lennon in the Little Quarter, this wall too afire, and here was
St. Nicholas Church: the Dome Fresco was in flames, the tall, am-
ber, painted glass ceiling melting, blackening—a tunnel of hell toward the sky. Then he and Anna were in Hradčany, looking down,
and all of Prague was ablaze. Anna called immediately for a doctor,
and soon that face was there, demanding Jiri's attention—white
coat, a man needing a shave. Asking Jiri for his location.

Location? Jiri said vaguely.

What state? the doctor said.

Jiri tried hard to think. Was he in the United States? Was he in a bunker in Prague, perhaps, or behind a barricade in the May uprising? He was in a cold sweat. He waited, frightfully, for the sound of bullets on steel and concrete.

There is a war going on, he said. *Everything is moving. Everything is on fire.*

Jiri? Everything is moving? the doctor said. *You're feeling dizzy?*

The walls are all moving, Jiri said.

Perhaps he is just very tired? Jiri heard the doctor ask Anna. *Perhaps he is dreaming?*

No, Doctor, Anna said. *Something is really wrong. This isn't like him. I know my husband.*

The doctor said: *Jiri, can you tell me who the president of the United States is?*

Jiri struggled; how could it be he couldn't know? *Roosevelt?* he said. That brought alarm to the eyes of the doctor.

He shakes his head at the memory. He turns on lamps, and at first he blinks his eyes as if he has come from a cave. It takes a good while for his eyes to adjust. Then here is the photograph, on the shelf above the ottoman, of his mother with her arm around his sister. Helena's eyes are merry with their mother's impatience, and now she has Jana laughing. Jiri leans closer, blinking, looks at their faces. *Hurry up, Jiri,* his mother says, trying again to be serious. *For heaven's sake, your sister will be late for work.*

———

One night in Prague in May 1945, Věra Kafková, Jana's friend, Jiri's old Lidice neighbor, immeasurably aged and with the insect-like blue number from Ravensbrück burned into her forearm, told Jiri of the last day she saw his sister and mother: *We were held three days in the school gymnasium in Kladno, and then they took the children away from their mothers. It was like something from Dante, honey, truly. You cannot believe. Then they began taking us away in trucks. Your mother and sister were in the next truck over from mine. I looked at your sister waiting there with that new, colorful bracelet on her wrist, and I thought she is too pretty a girl, too young a girl, to be going to a death camp.* Věra wept, and Jiri—realizing that as the Nazis came to Lidice his mother had given his sister his birthday gift—put his head in his hands and wept openly as well.

Through late nights in 1948, in the SS Archival Room at the Palace of Justice in Nuremberg—just one floor down from the army intelligence headquarters where he worked—Jiri had gone thoroughly through detention cards of Ravensbrück, Chelmno, Terezín. He found Marie Příhodová's name quickly—confirming what he'd known since the end of the war—imagined her in the back of that truck at Chelmno, perhaps comforting one of the younger children as the exhaust gas killed them. He'd had to leave the room, to walk outside on the ravaged streets of the city, rage in his throat.

There was no sign of his sister or mother in the long parade of identifying photographs and documents, a search of nearly a year; he spread out other SS photographs on the long wooden tables and bent over them with a magnifying glass—these carefully documented archives of annihilation, records for the master race—hoping to find the figures of Helena and his mother in them, a hint of where they might have been taken. His early inquiries to the

Western intelligence services, in 1945 and 1946, done through Dr. Kobera, had turned up nothing. He'd put advertisements in every major German and Czech publication starting in May 1945, and especially in the *Plzeň Examiner*, thinking that his mother might somehow have made it back to her old family home with his sister. He'd had flyers made with this photograph of Jana and Helena and plastered them all over the train stations of Czechoslovakia and Germany, Jana and Helena smiling beside so many other lost relatives, an ocean of faces, photographs, and messages fluttering sadly from these corridors, these walls of war-torn Europe: so many relatives lost to terror, the words *LAST SEEN* glaring from every flyer. *Helena Posseltová, age 18, and Jana Posseltová, age 38,* read Jiri's message, *of Lidice, Czechoslovakia, last seen in Kladno being taken into Nazi trucks on June 13, 1942. Please contact American Army Division, c/o Jiri Posselt, Palace of Justice, Nuremberg, Germany.*

He visited brothels throughout Munich on a tip that some Czech women, who had been brought to the Russian front as prostitutes for the German troops, were working now in Germany. *Perhaps Mother and Helena survived,* he'd thought, walking through the wet Munich streets one night in March 1947. *Perhaps the mistreatment of the soldiers made them crazy, and they no longer know who they are.* He showed prostitutes, and madams, and johns the picture of Helena and his mother and the bike, but no one recognized their faces.

The swastika still glows when he looks over. Hitler is there, looking down on the Danube, imagining the fires he will make. Following the girl named Stefanie, hovering in ghostly orbit around her, thinking of holding her in a place where she cannot escape him.

The sound of the first Lidice killing squad on June 10, 1942, is a terrifying crack through Jiri's stomach.

Didn't he see Tika today? Didn't he tell her about it? Did he tell her about the walls, the sound of the guns?

He remembers that he wanted to talk to her, to tell her of how the Nazis documented what they had done. How the Nazi title burned on the screen—*Instructive and Cultural Films*—and you saw the abandoned Lidice crest from Mayor Horák's office, three roses beneath a great green "L," and near it Jiri's father lay among the other murdered Lidice men, right arm thrown out across the ground, the hand in a fist, head turned to the sky. A Nazi moved among the bodies, pushed at his father's body with a jackboot. Jiri, watching the film for the first time in his Nuremberg office, had been unable to breathe in the clicking, film-sprocket darkness, had bent over to try to fill his lungs, and the sergeant running the projector for him had asked if they should continue.

Yes, Sergeant, keep it going, Jiri had said. *I need to see the rest of it.*

He had wanted to tell Tika, when they were walking by the roses at the Arboretum, whenever that was. Then he had looked over at her face and she seemed so happy that he had not wanted to bring his horror into the conversation.

Jiri turns off the light and goes clumsily to the bathroom, brushes teeth; he spits, and he is weeping, thinking of his father facing the guns. Of Marie in the truck, holding one of the crying children. That's what she would have done. *For God's sake, what happened with Mother and Helena?* He puts cold water into his mouth: That is better, cold water over his neck and face, for his head is aching. A towel. *Something normal, for God's sake. What was done was long done now and you know that if Mother and Helena had survived they would have found you, you would have found each other. Think of Markéta, married now—and perhaps there will be children still, a new generation, untouched by this madness. And think of Tika, enjoying her evening in freedom with a young man she loves—something Helena did not get to do. Think of these positive things.*

The bathroom light is bright; these orange-striped towels seem to glow. *The aching will disappear with just some aspirin. But is it all right to have aspirin with the Coumadin? I don't know, I don't want to wake Anna. Just some cold water to the forehead, then. Think of Markéta learning to ride her bike here on Trowbridge Street, Markéta looking over, quick smile: Look, Daddy. The colors of fall leaves all around her. Of visiting Markéta, of going to that all-night bookstore they have in Seattle, Markéta walking and breathing and the night-smell of the sea. Walking next to happy Markéta. The sound of gulls. In the warm bookstore your daughter pulled out books she wanted, Joan Larkin and Tobias Wolff and Gina Berriault. I will get them for you, honey. No, Daddy, you don't have to. I'm a big, rich girl now. Fending off her outstretched hand with cash: No, honey. Markéta's hand retreated with the bills and her eyes stared back, uncharacteristically shy.*

Jiri rubs the towel roughly over his cheekbones, his neck. Opens his shirt and cools his chest. Runs more cold on the cloth and holds it to his head awhile. He goes to bed, and in shadows Anna turns to him as he is sliding in. She comes close to him for a moment and he smells her hair, the closeness of her body.

"All right?" she says.

"Yes," he lies, and she is kissing his chest; sweet, poor Anna. She rolls back on her side and through the window you can see a bit of Trowbridge Street, a circle of tar beneath a streetlight, shadows of taut phone lines crossing that space.

II

FIVE

It is 1966.

Mrs. Dorling takes Simon and Jim out into the sun. Her feet are bare and tanned and she holds their hands. Her hand feels cool and smooth. They walk across the grass. Simon can feel the heat on his shoulders and back. Mrs. Dorling wanted them to wear hats and she has given them some of her own big straw ones and Jim and Simon laugh at each other, at how floppy the hats look. They hold the sides of the hats and say *wings* and *big ears* and beautiful Mrs. Dorling says, laughing with them, *Oh, you guys are so silly*. They reach a small fence and Mrs. Dorling points in.

Look at the sunflowers, she says. Look at how they turn to the sun.

I have them in my backyard, too, Simon says.

Aren't they pretty? Mrs. Dorling says.

Look at all the bees, Jim says. They kind of scare me.

You don't need to be scared, Mrs. Dorling says. She

kisses the throat, the side of the face of her son. Simon wishes she was doing that to him. Mrs. Dorling says, They're very busy. They're not so worried about stinging us.

Simon watches the bees hover and dip. They circle the big flowers. They light in the black orange center. He watches them crawl busily there. They twitch their wings.

You see these? Mrs. Dorling touches one of the floppy leaves of the sunflowers, and Simon is amazed that the bees do not bother her. Floppy, she says, like your crazy hats. These are called ray florets. They're here to attract the bees.

How do they know how to do all that? Simon says. Do the flowers have a brain?

Well, Mrs. Dorling pauses. Well God knows how to do that, honey.

The walk home for Simon that late afternoon is over the black hill. The tobacco grows there, green rows of leaves. Soon it will be picked and put into the barns and you will smell it all fall. He likes the smell of the tobacco. There are blackbirds near the tobacco barns, flying around in those trees at the edge of the field. The trees look like spiders against the red sky. Simon can see his house from here, single-story, the roof tin in places, the old barn. The road he is walking on doesn't do that thing anymore where it looks hot and wavy.

He is touching his new light green T-shirt. The other

shirt is tied around his waist—Mrs. Dorling tied it before he left, her arms stretching the sleeves around him,
making a firm knot.

He touches the sleeves of the T-shirt she bought
him, looks at his arm patches. This afternoon when she
came home from work Mrs. Dorling said, Boys, I have a
fun project for you. See these T-shirts? I got them for
you at Aster's. They are just like shirts that our guys
wear in Vietnam. Now, here are some patches for you to
pick from. We'll iron whatever you want on the sleeves.
Simon picked the air force, because of the star and
stripes. You'll be an air force sergeant, Mrs. Dorling told
him. Jim wanted the navy SEALs. Mrs. Dorling stood
over Simon and showed him how to line up the patch
on the T-shirt sleeve. He could feel her very close to
him. Her hand helped guide his and together they
pushed the iron, and then there it was, blue stripes
against the green, like magic. In the late sun, walking,
he looks at his patches on each sleeve. He touches his
patches.

He thinks of his sisters looking at the patches on his
new shirt. Faith will say something good about his air
force stars and stripes, he is sure of it. She is older
than him, and Cindy is younger. Dexter will just keep
sitting and watching television, and when Mom comes
home pretty late, she and Dexter will go under the
blanket in front of the television, laughing. Simon will
be asleep then, so maybe his mother will see the
patches tomorrow.

At home Dexter is in front of the television, as Simon

knew he'd be. Dexter has a scraggly beard and small dark eyes and his boots are on the table. Simon's mother will tell him not to do that. Dexter is pretty much home all day and usually he makes macaroni and cheese for everyone for supper even though Faith has learned how to do it and Simon likes it when she does because then Dexter doesn't even come into the kitchen. Simon hears Majo, their Irish setter, barking from where she is chained to the barn. Dexter chews on a fingernail and looks at Simon just for a second and then keeps watching, and someone is saying, *I'll give you the money or you can just choose what is behind door number three. Your choice. Okay, folks, she is going for door number three!* And the audience is applauding and then the voice is saying, *And what do we have there? We have a donkey cart.* And a funny horn is blowing and the audience is groaning and applauding and laughing and Simon would like to go and see the donkey cart but he does not want to be around Dexter. When seven o'clock comes *Batman* will be on and Dexter always lets the three of them watch when he goes into the garage to work on his motorcycle. Simon runs up the hallway now. He is Batman, chasing the Riddler! He bursts into his sisters' door and Faith is folding some clothes and they scream and Cindy laughs and Faith says, Who gave you the really cool shirt? And Simon says, Oh, hm, I got it from Mrs. Dorling, we made it at her house. And Faith says with wide eyes, She gave it to you? And Simon says, Mm-hm, and Faith says, I have this friend, Mandy, and her mom does iron-on stuff with these flower patches and I'd like to learn how to do that. And Cindy says, *Iron on!* And Simon takes a towel from Faith's pile and folds it around his neck like a cape and points and says, Now, Robin, after the Riddler! And he runs down the hallway and out across the television and Dexter says, God*damn*it Simon and Simon runs back and reminds himself to just run into the kitchen instead of the living room, and back in the girls' room Cindy wants to be Batgirl but she has stubbed her toe and is crying, and that's no good to be around, Faith will make her feel better, and Simon and Robin race back down the hallway, into the kitchen, which is now Gotham City, all these buildings around, all these lights. And in the girls' room again Faith says, Did you find the Riddler? I'm Batgirl, and the Riddler's got a debt to pay and Faith's fist is in the air and they are racing down the hallway and Simon goes across the television again, feels that his sister has stopped behind him, knows what he's done just as the couch creaks, and Dexter grabs his shoulder, spins him around, steps on both his feet, Simon looking up, up at that mountain of angry Dexter, chest in red shirt and then beard and the dark eyes, looking angry but like Dexter might laugh too, and the audience beside Simon on the color television is shrieking with laughter. Dexter says, Go into another room, Simon! And Simon is unable to move because those feet are crushing his, it hurts so much, he struggles, he falls in terror onto his haunches, his two sisters watching him, wide-eyed, from the doorway.

Can't fucking move now, after fucking running every-

where? Too fucking bad, Simon. Weird eyes of Dexter, Simon swallows hard. *Okay, boy.* The feet release and Simon falls, scrambles, gets up again and runs past his sisters, throwing himself down the hallway, already crying with the terror of it, into his mother's towel in the bathroom, burying himself in its smell, the smell of coconuts. *Wait a minute you little fuck. You fucking bother me through the whole fucking show, can't fucking sit still, going and fucking going.* Here the voice gets lost in a guttural rage and the boy tries to turn and run past that huge body, to run into the evening, down the steps, outside maybe to Mrs. Dorling's place, because he knows what is coming, but the rough hand has him by the shirt, flings him down the hallway toward the kitchen. The hand opens the door to the garage and Simon gets the bag of rice from the shelf out there and gives it to Dexter and watches while Dexter pours it onto the linoleum floor. Dexter takes a long time doing it, spreading it thin, and Simon feels in his stomach like he might throw up, he might scream. His sisters are gone now, ordered outside; he is grateful, does not want them near, to see Dexter pointing at the floor, saying, *Okay, kid, pray.*

Simon kneels, his hands clasped in front of him; he is supposed to ask for forgiveness, *because I do not think of others.* And the rice is not so bad right away—you almost believe that this time it will be different, you're used to it now, it won't hurt so bad—but then it is digging through his jeans, burning, and Dexter leaves the room and Simon lets the tears come, then tells himself

Batman wouldn't be stupid and cry, but he can't help it, and he brushes the tears from his face but when he moves his arms it makes his knees feel even more like they are on pins of fire and then his back aches horribly and he weeps openly from the pain of every time he shifts to make his back better there is the new pain at the knees, and he tries to keep his hands clasped before him because if Dexter catches him not praying it will just go longer, and he weeps with his anger at Dexter. Dexter turns up the television loudly in the next room, that audience laughing and yelling out door numbers, and Simon tries to think about the laughter and about what that donkey and cart might have looked like. Faith and Cindy are thinking of him outside, he knows they are; they are maybe down at the pond near the tobacco field where the bullfrogs in the evening start making so much noise. Faith will cry, but she will keep Cindy busy.

Fifteen minutes by the kitchen clock now: Simon hears the dog barking during the quiet TV moments so maybe Faith and Cindy are throwing Majo sticks, maybe Majo is running like she does, diving from the land to the water, catching the stick before it splashes. *Oh God my knees.* Simon might run for the door—but he won't make it across the room, the way his knees are, and Dexter will hit him then, and he'll spend more time on the rice. The cookie jar by the toaster has a smiling brown face, and Simon stares at it, thinks of it alive, a cartoon with arms moving, hands waving, eyebrows raising with that smile. Simon takes a chance, drops his

hands onto his thighs, then onto the floor, lifting himself a little, and that is so much better until his arms
cannot hold out any longer. He takes a deep breath and
puts his knees down and his hands on his hips and his
knees flame up and he moves his hands so that they
hold the small of his back; he grits his teeth, because
the pins are so much worse now. He listens all the time
for the creaking of the couch. Twenty minutes. The
show ends, the host wishing everyone good luck, *hoping
all your deals are happy ones,* and the TV lowers and Simon wipes his tears, fiercely, quickly, his knees
flaming—you try to stop the crying when you hear the
TV lower, the couch creaks, and he puts his hands before him, clasped, and there is the relief of Dexter's
footsteps at the doorway. *Okay, kid, sweep it up,* Dexter
says, and Simon rises painfully, gasping, brushes rice
from his knees, the palms of his hands, gets the broom
and scoop from the corner, near his mother and Dexter's
bedroom. He can see the edge of the bed there, the
window looking onto the driveway. They do that thing in
there, sometimes they leave the door open. He sweeps
the rice, every bit of it with Dexter watching from a
kitchen chair, the television still low, the magical
sounds of *Bewitched* coming on. Sweeps and scoops
into a small paper bag, then goes to the garage for the
shovel and takes the bag into the yard, into the trees at
the edge of the field behind the house, Dexter watching
from the back door. Simon buries the bag so that his
mother will never find the rice. When he is finished he
puts the shovel back into the cement-smelling garage

and does not look at Dexter as he goes by him. He goes into the house and down the hallway quickly to his bedroom. He shuts his door, locks it, throws himself on the bed. Dexter's voice seems to vibrate through that wood. *Spew that fucking nervous energy through this house all you want, kid. We'll make sure you spend as much time on that floor. What kind of life have you had? You just do whatever the fuck you want, huh? You just run all over the fucking house, like nobody else is alive. Well you won't do that shit with me. Fuck!* The door bangs with Dexter's fist, and Simon feels it like a jump off a high place in his stomach, and his heart pounds in his ears. Then the footsteps are leaving and the television is loud again.

I wish you weren't alive, Simon thinks to himself. He lies facedown on his bed and holds his chest and throat tightly so as not to weep: he will not let Dexter hear him weeping again. But it comes; he tries to swallow it, his stomach jerking for a long time. After a while he can hear the cicadas through the window. It is all right for them to listen; he has no secrets from them. His mother's sunflowers brush against the screen of the window. *She* and *she* and *she* and *she* they say. They are always awake; even when night comes it is like they have small fires of the sun in them. It is all right for them to listen, too.

His mother's punishments for his energy are different; she does only, she says, what her father did to her, *and somehow we have to get you to calm down, Simon!* When he runs feverishly through the house, forgetting himself, she will catch him and make him walk the same pattern that he has run in, sometimes one hundred evolutions, making him count. Faith is usually playing Go Fish at the kitchen table with Cindy, and she watches her brother sadly as he paces. Sometimes it really looks like Faith is going to cry. All that walking is boring, and you want to scream, because other than counting off you are not allowed to talk, but it is not so hard and crazy like Dexter's punishments. Simon keeps note of everything he passes until he can close his eyes and recite, in a whisper, *Old clock with pendulum, hallway dark brown rug, Mama in her picture with Cindy and Faith, me in the yellow baseball shirt, mirror, turn into my room, turn around, hallway, kitchen with Faith and Cindy playing cards, paper roll on wall, kitchen clock, refrigerator, phone, old clock with pendulum . . .* The naming of things makes it a little better. Dexter occasionally looks up from the couch, the television blaring before him. Sometimes without thinking about the rule not to talk Simon will start reciting out loud, and Dexter will tell him, *Goddamnit, Simon, say it to yourself.*

Simon never mentions to his mother how Dexter forces him onto the rice. Dexter has told him and his sisters that he will just find worse ways to punish Simon if they tell, and they believe him. But one evening, when Simon's knees have broken open and bled, and Dexter has gone to work at the bar and his mother is home from her waitressing job early, Simon is in his underwear walking to the bathroom and his mother says, *Honey, what happened?* and he says, *I fell today, in the woods,* and Faith comes out of her bedroom with Cindy behind her, and Faith has her chin stuck out and she says, Tell her. And their mother's face darkens and she says, Tell me what and Cindy's eyes grow large behind Faith and Faith tells all of it, and leads their mother out to the edge of the forest with a flashlight and shovel to prove it, digging everything up, the disintegrating bags and insects and the bloody rice.

There is a holy row when Dexter returns home. From his bed, full of hope and fear, Simon hears it—Dexter's voice rising in anger, *Fucking lying kids;* his mother more angry, a thunderstorm in the house, saying twice the words Dexter does until Dexter is not talking much at all. Simon hears the door slam, and he hopes that means Dexter is leaving (maybe leaving for good!?); he only breathes better when he hears Dexter's truck slamming through gears, turning out of the driveway. Then there is the sound of the night and Simon sleeps, full of soaring joy, comforted by these sunflowers at his window screen with their sun fires in their heads. They say *she* and *she* and *she* and *she.*

The sunflowers wake him much later, scratching at the window.

She and *she* and *she* and *she.*

The moon makes a stripe over Simon's legs. The cicadas sing outside. Simon hears laughter: his mother. He rises and goes to the kitchen. At the end of the kitchen is the bedroom door, slightly open. On the kitchen table is the blue square of paper, white traces of powder. Simon goes to the bedroom door, hears that breathing that he has heard many times before, his mother and Dexter doing the thing. He glances in, moonlight spilling across the bed, where his mother's dirty feet are across Dexter's back, the rest of her under him, and he hears her voice whispering, *Oh God that's good oh my fucking God,* and Simon turns back and for a moment he leans against the doorjamb, feeling heat in his face and having great trouble catching a breath. Outside Majo begins barking incessantly, knowing that something within their home is very, very wrong.

G host-Man is struck dumb here, holding on to his grocery cart, staring, warning voices going off in his head but unable to stop gawking like an idiot at Alison Tiner's hands on the pliable bag of rice, and he turns quickly to the display of instant rice himself, looks hard at the bright boxes. Alison Tiner is walking up the aisle, the rice in her cart. The benevolent huckster, Uncle Ben, suggests that everything will be all right if you just cook the right meal, *100% Naturally Seasoned, Trusted for over Fifty Years, "Perfect Every Time."* Ghost-Man wipes the wetness from his cheeks with his hand. Down the next aisle he grasps cans of chili and Alison Tiner is just turning at the end of the taco fixings; she picks up mustard in the condiments section there and then she is gone and Ghost-Man moves his grocery cart over the smooth, brown-flecked tiles and makes the turn and here is the fruit, the palate of colors, and Ghost-Man gets near Alison Tiner and soon both of them are looking over apples, bright hard red. She does not notice him, for there are many people here; Ghost-Man smells the earth in these apples, smells Kentucky, sees beautiful Mrs. Dorling, her bare, tanned feet in grass, her slender wrists. Alison Tiner turns and pushes ahead, past the display refrigerator with its pasta and pesto and when Ghost-Man sees her again, as he pushes his cart with chili cans and Macintosh reds and a small bottle of soy milk, she is down at the salad dressings, considering. *You consider, woman: your face growing older, your personality hidden all of those years ago by the levity of youth, now the face lined when you concentrate, angry crow's-feet at the eyes. A fat-free dressing, lite ranch, for the feast! For the food that will draw your man in.*

There is a question of female judgment, Ghost-Man knows, in everything. *She* decides whether to let a man penetrate her, unless he forces her—and then he should simply die—but otherwise it is her judgment that rocks the universe. *She* is the great judge, the regulator; will her man, will mankind, be civil? Or will he get what he wants with his simple brutality? *She* decides with *her* actions! *She* can make mountains fall, wars begin, children laugh. Alison Tiner gathers: chicken to cook with her rice, green beans in butter sauce that she will microwave, candles to illuminate the face of her lover just minutes before she gives her body to him. Ghost-Man imagines her lighting these, a sweep of match, quick outbreath of flame. Blue fire in her eyes as, protecting the match with a cupped hand, she moves forward to the candlewicks.

SIX

A t the Holy Mackerel in Central Square, Monkey's Fist is pounding through "Money," Jesse's and Elijah's voices doubling, screaming on the vocal. Tika has them in the Leica's frame, shooting from the back of the club, near the bar, and she suddenly lowers the camera and watches the whole scene because it is magnificent—the five members of the band playing tight, sweating under the tracers, twenty minutes into their set. There will be three bands up tonight and Monkey's Fist is on first. The Holy Mackerel is not a big club, but it is very crowded; there is a stage, a bar behind Tika, walls and floors and pole supports washed in heavy gray paint. The walls near the booths are decorated with stills of 1960s television shows, especially *Batman;* and on the wall over the stage, lit by spotlights and framed by gaudy velour curtains, there is a large mural of a buxom blond woman, in lingerie, straddling a mackerel. Over the head of the woman is a shining halo.

Tika estimates that three hundred are here; behind her she hears people shouting for "one Johnnie Walker please and a pitcher, thanks man," and "Yes, I want a toasted almond and a Scotch," and Jesse's bass is booming through the Marshall stacks, and Tika braces herself on the floor and feels Jesse and the band through her legs and she raises the Leica and through her wide-angle telephoto lens Jesse is there close with his good face and his eyes squeezed shut behind Buddy Holly glasses, singing with his intensity into the microphone, a lock of hair falling over his fore-head and sweat glistening at his temples. Bracing her elbows, she frames the shot. His black T-shirt reads, in bright letters, *No More Land Mines,* and his cherry Spector bass is slung across his waist, his right hand slapping at the heavy strings. Tika fires off three rapid pictures. She is using Kodak 3200 film, pushed to 64; soon she will need more, and there are the two rolls in her case in the dressing room. She thinks of the sumptuous feel of Dennis Stock's photographs of Miles Davis, the energy of the Hendrix series that Baron Wolman shot in San Francisco, in 1968. The strange, stark sense of Elliot Erwitt's work in the late 1950s and 1960s. She has been keeping all of these artists in her mind as, through clubs and beerfests and at radio shows this summer, she has made her por-traits of her boyfriend's band.

She lowers the camera to her chest and makes her way to a cor-ner booth, the floor sticky here, leans against the table. The group in the booth, three guys, two girls, college age, glance up and nod and smile, drunk already, and Tika nods and apologizes, though she knows they cannot hear her. She unclips the wide-angle lens and takes from her jacket a leather cylinder, a Leitz Tel 4 T, 200 mm, and fits and clips it into the Leica. She puts the lens cap onto the wide angle and slips the lens into the cylinder and nods to the group again—one of the boys tries to say something to her, looking at her as if he remembers her, to extend a hand, but Tika acts as if she doesn't notice and walks forward to a gray-washed pole. She braces herself against it, and through the Leica, bright and close, Eric Sheff on the raised Tama drum set whacks the skins with controlled, rhythmic fury. Eric wears dark glasses and a black shirt, and his arms are fully tattooed; his mouth is slightly open. Tika catches now, on his wrist, rising and falling in rhythm, the cloth skull-and-crossbones bracelet he wears on his right arm. He is a very sweet, studied guy, finishing a degree at the New England Conservatory. He is a madman on the drums—and the vibration of them goes through Tika's bones.

Jesse swears his throat is always going to tear out on this song, he puts so much into it: *Every note of every song of every performance,* he always says, *we're gonna give it everything, because you never know who's out there in the audience.* Eric and Pug "Mozart" Hines and Kerig Scott, the lead guitarist, sing on the choruses now—Jesse screams, *"Well now give me money!"* and they sing, *"That's what I want!"* Jesse screams, *"I wanna be free!"* and the whole band sings, *"That's what I want!"* Elijah's long brown hair is swept behind him, his Rickenbacker muscling out the chords, and beside him Pug pounds the Yamaha keys, wearing a dark long-sleeved Superman shirt, his teeth showing in his perpetual grin, his own glasses flashing under stage lights; the notes of the Yamaha harmonize with Kerig's distorted lead guitar.

Tika moves in closer as the song hits a crescendo, the lights now an intense white, then yellow, then blue. She braces her legs and watches through the camera her Jesse. Fists are in the air before him, and many naked female arms reach for his shins. *Fine,* she thinks. *He's good-looking, my Jesse, with his wonderful wide shoulders, his long throat—that will sell CDs.* Jesse looks over as Pug pounds into a last solo, and Jesse's beautiful vein runs up his forearm, and sweat is shining on his jaw. Tika shoots four and she is done and walking through the forest of bodies, a tight path smelling of whiskey and marijuana and perfume. She nods to the large security guard, Neil—a man nearly as wide as this battered door—and steps into the back hallway, toward the dressing room, forty-watt bulbs just lighting her way.

In the small dressing room the music is just slightly more subdued: Jesse's bass and Eric's bass drum still thump solidly through the cement-block wall. She sits on the old couch, picks up Jesse's beaten leather coat (*Harley-Davidson Motor Cycles,* says the emblem on the back of the jacket, *Established 1903, Milwaukee, WI*), and smoothes it onto her lap. She smells now of smoke and alcohol, smells this even on the back of her hand, her white rope bracelet, and she loves it, this smoke-filled rock-and-roll world of her boyfriend; she sets the camera, her leather case, beside her. She listens to the end of the song, four whacks of the drums, the band together on the final, sustained note, the applause and whistling like wind. On the wall, in frames, Batman and Robin race to the gleaming Batmobile, the intricate Batcave with its computers all around them. In another still, Adam West stands at Wayne Manor, at a party, wearing trim slacks, a collegiate sweater, holding a glass of wine; above that, Batman strikes hard at a thug, a sweep of fist, with the cartoon caption *Pow!* across the top of the picture.

A tuxedo hangs on the bathroom shower stall: Pug will change into it after showering, and play a late night gig at a private party—Gershwin and Miles Davis and Thelonious Monk. Kerig Scott has invited the rest of them to meet his new girlfriend at the Club Isis in Copley Place—there is an official opening party going on all week, and the place will be open until four. Eric said he was sorry, he already had a date himself, and Jesse whispered to Tika, *We probably should,* and Tika nodded enthusiastically. Some of her friends at Emerson and at Standish's Pub have been buzzing about the new club. It is anybody's guess if Elijah will go, as screwed up as he is over a relationship he lost in July; he's not much for hanging out lately.

She drops in the Kodak roll, leads it onto the sprockets, closes the back of the Leica and turns the thumb lever, spooling the film in; she faintly hears Jesse's voice joking with the crowd, and many voices yelling and hands clapping. Eric hits a couple of notes. The song they are about to do is the one Tika has brought to all the college radio stations. Monkey's Fist will make it, Tika is sure of it: sure that they are on the verge of something big. She has watched her Jesse working, night after night, spread out on the worn Oriental rug of his Jamaica Plain apartment, papers—songs in the making—all around him, his Gibson plugged into the Roland digital recorder that he has borrowed from the music store. Tika helps where she can: She has taken the photographs of the group that have been in the *Boston Phoenix* and *The Noise* and *Stuff at Night* and that get plastered to lampposts throughout Cambridge and Boston, next to flyers for all the other current groups, Mistle Thrust and Doctor Frog and Dragstrip Courage and Eve Was Framed. Tika changes guitar strings, sometimes runs the Roland for Jesse when he wants to put down a final version of a song. A few days ago she helped him replace the S-pipe on the 1994 Chevy van that the group owns, crawling under with him and holding up the pipe while he soldered. They were in the garage the band rents, motorcycles and instrument boxes all around them, everything lit by hanging lightbulbs, an *Elvis* license plate nailed to the inside of the door. Jesse had said, *Honey you're doing too much, you shouldn't be doing all of this,* but secretly Tika knows that he loves having her there by his side, that she is not the kind of girl who is afraid of anything, of any work.

Three months ago Kascha was on *The Late Show with David Letterman;* maybe she'll know someone there who can help launch Monkey's Fist when they get the CD out. And there are all the parties Kascha goes to, all the producers she rubs elbows with. Kascha has already said she wants to help, that there are two producers in Los Angeles she thinks would be interested, and Tika has asked her sister to start looking into it. But Tika won't say anything to Jesse unless she gets some solid leads—she knows from Kascha that few show business people deliver what they promise.

She finishes winding in the film, slips the camera case over her shoulder, and steps into the hallway again, down to the stage door. The overhead bulbs emit an ethereal light; just a little while ago, when the band went on at nine, Tika kissed Jesse in the hallway here and wished him luck, then kissed his throat and held him close, and the others passed by, joking that someone should get a room, and Jesse, grinning, went through the door with them and she heard the audience in rousing applause as the band strapped on their instruments in the darkness.

She goes through the same stage door now, stepping through the shadows, wires on the floor, guitar cases, beaten-up equipment cases with block stenciling, *Monkey's Fist* and *Pug Mozart,* here behind this drawn curtain. She steps to the small slip of opening in the heavy velour and here is the band in profile; Eric hits a time on the sticks, and then the others are with him, and the lights intensify, tracers following the shoulders of Jesse and Elijah, blue, yellow, and red, Eric's head above in a halo, and Tika can see Pug's face, anticipating, looking up at Eric, as they time the intro. The

audience is applauding already, recognizing, whistling, and Jesse's
bass hits, and Elijah is singing.

> I see you in the city street
> Late one night where raindrops meet
> In water lit by neon like a fire
> Woman you are everywhere
> And in this endless night we share
> Your memory's burnin' through me like a wire

Elijah started writing the song after a late night walk this summer through Boston. Jesse had told Tika about Elijah's breakup,
the next night in bed on Trowbridge Street, just after helping Elijah
finish the piece; the woman, twenty-nine years old to Elijah's
twenty-five, was upset with what she called Elijah's nomadic, Bohemian life. Tika remembered her with Elijah at a party in Brookline, where Monkey's Fist was being courted by a local producer
(Jesse later decided the man was a con artist): Tika'd seen a tall,
very good-looking woman, blond and with a burgundy silk cardigan
and pants, a silk scarf about her neck, holding a wineglass and
leaning against a besotted Elijah. The party had been filled with local rock-and-roll musicians and their girlfriends; there was a famous filmmaker there and a broadcaster who had gone from the
local Boston market to national celebrity as a game-show host. It
was one of those gatherings that was, to Tika's mind, more about
people trying to make you jealous, to make your own accomplishments pale next to their supposed greatness. Tika always felt uncomfortable around such egos. But Elijah's lover had seemed in her
element, and her eyes were full of play, and she had laughed with
her long throat and Elijah had watched her all night. In bed, Tika

told Jesse that there were some women who would like the *image* of what the guys were doing—who would enjoy seeing themselves in the midst of that image, for a while—at parties with the unconventional and famous, draped around a man like Elijah; those women, Tika said, wanted their men eventually in a box, and Jesse had nodded. *Balls in a cage,* he'd said. Apparently, the woman realized that Elijah was into music for the long haul—it wasn't just some fashionable phase—and it wasn't long after, on a weekend at some resort, that she dumped him. Elijah hadn't been able to let loose of her, Jesse'd said. *Sometimes,* Jesse said, *he drives up north to Newburyport where she lives and just freaking checks out who's going in and out of her house. He even watches her go in and out of work. He's sort of going nuts. We're still trying to pull him out of it.*

Elijah's head is bowed now, his long brown hair falling forward, a few discernible faces of the audience around his figure. Tika wonders if he still thinks of the woman as he plays, of her place up there by the ocean and the way he's stood there, watching her home from the protection of trees. *There are always these ghosts,* she thinks, imagining Jiri's haunted face when she came to the door this evening. *We're always in orbit around a phantom something.* Now Jesse goes forward to the microphone to sing on the chorus, all of these eyes watching him and Elijah together:

> And the storm winds blow
> They're going right through me
> 'Cause baby I'm a ghost
> Of the man I used to be

Tika watches the circle of audience eyes: thinks of Elijah and the woman he still loves. Then of a winter day at the Museum of

Fine Arts last year—snow on the eaves of the wonderful old buildings and fog in the streets and going in with Jesse to see John
Lennon's guitar. The old Rickenbacker behind glass, a circle of
people staring in awe, thinking of the Beatles and history, each lost
in some memory of their own. *In orbit around a phantom something.*

She removes the telephoto lens and puts it in her case; she
reaches in and comes up with a Spiratone fish-eye lens that she
snaps quickly onto the Leica, and steps toward the back of the
stage, so that she has all of the members of the band in the shot:
Eric warped toward the ceiling, lights raining. The circle of shining, audience eyes. The song closes and the thunder of applause
goes up and Tika begins shooting, capturing this ring of human
light.

SEVEN

Jiri dreams that he is in some old colonial home. It is morning and there is a restful forest surrounding the house and Jesse and Tika have quietly been talking and they apologize for waking him up. *Not at all,* Jiri says; the sun stretches golden over the old wooden walls and immediately he is engaged in a discussion and Lord! how he can talk. He tells them about southern Bavaria and sailing on Bodensee and how the countryside around Immenstadt is emerald green in the spring sun. How one fall he swam completely across Lake Tergensee and how very cold and refreshing it was; that was 1951, and he and Anna had been married almost three years. They skied high in the Alps, at Garmisch-Partenkirchen, and took the train back to Munich. He'd put in many intense hours on the job that winter, for all of the intelligence services were trying to catch up with a character they called *Duch,* the Demon-spirit, an East German SSD assassin who was killing exiled Czech and Hungarian leaders with the use of a hydrogen-cyanide gun. The Duch was never found.

I never found my mother and sister, he tells his young friends, *and*

the world forgot about Czechoslovakia. In the films that came out of
his old country he saw how decrepit, how gray and worn the buildings and cobblestoned streets were. The faces of his countrymen
seemed without hope. There was the brief sunshine, the possibility, of Dubček. Then in 1969, after the Soviets rolled into Prague,
he and Anna decided to leave Europe. *I couldn't watch things disappear anymore,* he says.

In this old, sunlit-filled home Tika and Jesse look at him with
great respect, and Jiri knows they are amazed, as he is, at how he
can talk: it is as if he is lifting off the ground, beginning to fly.
There is so much that he has wanted to talk with Tika about! And
now as he thinks of it, he realizes he shall soon be able to work
again for the Guild—to take the train to the business district, and
the buildings of blue glass will be above him, and he will be free
again, walking with his briefcase as he did last March, when he last
went there on the T, snow melting, sunshine in the city, the breath
of cool air.

And then he is awake, in the darkness beside his wife, and he
can think with the same old speed, but he knows he would not be
able to bring his thoughts fluidly to his lips. For a moment he feels
he might choke with the sadness of it, of what he has lost in the
moment from sleep to waking. He snaps the covers away from himself, thinks: *So. I'll heal this somehow, damn it.*

Marjorie Legnini told him early, after he lost the speech, that
the writing gives him greater access to his thoughts, that whatever
the path is between the brain and the mouth is eased with the writing process. The doctors don't quite know why this is, she said, but
she had seen it work many times. *So.* He rises and puts on his flannel, threadbare robe over a T-shirt; he gets into khakis, slippers. He
takes his cane. Anna sighs, hardly conscious, irritated at her hus-

band's nightly restlessness. He can walk ceaselessly at night these days—through the flat, or to check the Buick for fluids, or up and down the sidewalk before their building. Jiri goes into the library and turns on the light and sits on the ottoman, the window in the nook before him slightly opened to screens. He picks up the memory book, unclips a pen from its cover. The glass is a glossy black stretch, and his fingers are reflected there, turning the pages, the leaves above a collection of dark pressing shapes.

The swastika across the room is less prominent in the light. No hovering now, just a flat symbol on the spine of an old book. Jiri watches it, feels the early fall air circulating from the opened windows of the apartment. Then he begins to write. *It is a sound of laughter that he focuses on—a young woman's laughter—a tourist, perhaps, in this late afternoon. He is in Linz, a few years ago, with Anna, on a stopover to Prague.* It is winter. The yellow, red, and white medieval houses surround them, a frosting of snow on the red-tiled roofs. Niches in the walls parade intricately carved angels and saints, balconies that in summer will weep with flowers and plants. The windows of the baroque shops are frosted with snow and ice hangs from the archways and it is cold, some wind blowing, snow drifting sometimes through the street horizontally. A few people walk about, their footsteps and voices echoing in the strange winter silence. Jiri hears the woman's laughter, and he thinks of a similar sound, ninety-five years before. The anguished boy standing in this very place, understanding that Stefanie cannot be his. Jiri feels he is walking in a graveyard of millions.

He and Anna come to an old dance hall. There are wide steps of marble up from the street, massive balustrades adorned at the entrance by carved lions. The place is being refurbished now to house a business, but Jiri imagines Adolf Hitler walking up these wide steps to one of the large windows. The young Hitler staring in at the dancers: men in uniform, women in wide, sweeping dresses. Faces in there of joy; light from the chandeliers intensely warm on the floorboards. And there, in the arms of a lieutenant—one of those who offered her a flower on the Promenade—dances the extraordinary girl Stefanie. She has a white-gloved hand on the lieutenant's shoulder. Adolf Hitler stands at the window, watching, annihilated.

Jiri is writing in Czech now, remembering words that President Havel wrote and that Jiri translated, sitting in this same chair, ten years before. *Zločinci zůstali na svobodě a volně se pohybovali mezi námi předstírali že jsou čestní lidé dvacátého. Století, kteří nevěří ve zločiny. The demons have been turned loose and go about . . . confronting this modern world with machine guns in their hands, they believe themselves to be instruments of providence: after all, they are merely meting out punishment in accordance with the ancient prophecy about the desecrator of their Golden Temple.*

Hitler at the window plans his punishments for the world. Even fate will bend to his wishes! He can trust in his own will, if nothing else. There is relief in this. Wind dashes a spray of snow all around him. He can hear the laughter, the grand music through the glass, but in this moment, filled with his plans, he can convince himself he is above such things.

Now a car rushes by quickly on Trowbridge Street, a white hiss through fallen leaves. Jiri sees the motion behind his reflection, his fingers tight with the pen. He writes the word *annihilation,* thinks of how Adolf Hitler murdered everything he, Jiri, loved. There was a girl named Alena during the war (or this was how Jiri knew her—you never knew the true name of anyone in your Resistance group, so that if captured by the Gestapo you would not betray the others). She was a long-limbed, older Czech girl who took his virginity one night not long after he joined Kobera's Resistance cell. He thinks of Alena now and how her face looked above him in the night; he was fifteen. They were in the loft of a safe house, a stable in Veltrusy, and stars were bright beyond the dark of her, through the opened loft hatch; she too had lost her family to the Nazis. She'd dug her hands into his chest and pressed herself onto him, and her lips went to his ear. He'd swooned at how fierce and insistent a woman's body could be, *nature* could be: He'd been indoctrinated into this new world.

It was on the next day—wasn't it? Jiri looks down at the memory book but finds no answers there, for this is the first time he has written of Alena—that they had rescued a Jewish physicist from a cattle train en route to Terezín: Alena was there for that, he knows. And she had been by his side when they had, in the same week, blown an ammunition depot on the outskirts of Plzeň. A few days later she and the two others from the Resistance group were caught cutting phone lines, and they had chosen to fight and die rather than be captured. Alena took a bullet to the throat. Jiri wept when he heard, turned away from Dr. Kobera and stared out another window of yet another safe house, thinking of the girl he'd hardly known and of how those last moments for her must have been. Dr. Kobera was quiet but stayed in the room; clearly he'd guessed that Jiri liked the girl, though perhaps he did not know that they had made love. Jiri's leader put on coffee, watched Jiri a few moments and said, with his firm voice, *We are living in the time of the demon, Jirko. I have lost loved ones, too, and in horrible ways. It is a tremendous tragedy. But you must listen to me. You are exhausted and in grief, but you must return to thinking coldly. Activity will help you out of this.* Jiri swore he would kill every Nazi he saw, just give him the chance. *There are many more of them than us,* Dr. Kobera said. *Musíme být opatrní a musíme rozhodnout, které bitvy bojovat. We must be intelligent and pick our battles.*

Jiri gets up and goes into the kitchen and makes coffee. He sits at the kitchen table and continues with the writing. He writes into the night. He remembers returning to Lidice in the summer of 1945, the Nazi barbed wire that surrounded his desecrated village gone and only a large cross on the spot where his father and the other men had been murdered. They had been buried there by a detail of Jews from Terezín. There was dander blowing through the air and nothing else but wind and grass. All else completely eliminated—if it were not for the cross, it might have been that Lidice never existed. Jiri knelt and touched the ground and wept for his father and all the Lidice men.

Jiri writes of being a boy, his father looking with him into a telescope, the two of them exclaiming at the bright, Copernicus crater on the moon, at the rings of Saturn and glowing red Mars. Of his father shot, dead eyes toward the sky, hand in a fist. Marie in the gas truck, Alena shot through the throat.

And Jana and Helena where? Where disappeared into the demon's fire?

EIGHT

In Harvard Square the fire performers seem to make the night sky dance over the buildings. The torches spin, flames with blue black hearts; faces crowd around, lit in wonder, the orange light and shadows tremble on brick sidewalk and walls. Jesse's arm is over Tika's shoulder, and Tika holds those fingers, feeling her lover's body close. He has showered at the Holy Mackerel and now wears a T-shirt, the Harley jacket, jeans. He looks good this way, his hair catching the lights of the shops; his body feels strong, something to hold on to. Tika runs her fingers, hard, over his knuckles and the guitar-callused tips of his fingers, kneads the base of his thumb.

There are many people, so many people, in Harvard Square now: cars moving slowly, desperately, through the main intersection as large groups of pedestrians cross. Tika and Jesse walk up the sidewalk past Warburton's Bakery and the Discovery Channel store, and Tika gives three dollars to a homeless advocate and slides the *Spare Change* issue she receives into her camera case. They duck into Standish's—a mob of people waiting at the entrance, so that Tika decides only to wave to her friend and coworker, Pentti Kim, who is just coming back from seating a couple, and Pentti waves and then with her thumb and pinkie raises an imaginary phone to her ear and mouths the words *Call me*. Tika gives a thumbs-up and she and Jesse step on the sidewalk again. Here is a flood of teenagers, mostly in black. One teenage girl has heavy dark mascara, hair clenched and dyed black and pink, nose and lips pierced. She wears a black, long-sleeved shirt that says, *I like you, I'll kill you last*. A pretty woman in a business suit steps by the teenagers, and now an older man with a beard, clutching a beaten leather briefcase. Tika holds Jesse's hand, watches her boyfriend's shoulders in front of her, the tangle of his still-damp hair, and all around them is the human river with its sounds: footsteps and radios and cars honking and conversation and the guitars. The old clock outside the Harvard Coop reads 10:38, and above it, over the eighteenth-century buildings of the university, a jet is winking in the black sky.

They cross the street to the island, to Out of Town News, and while Jesse looks over an issue of *Musician*, Tika picks up *Rolling Stone*. She feels the heat of a man staring at her and turns and he is older, perhaps in his late thirties, with a mustache and long hair and tweed jacket, and he quickly switches his interest back to a magazine. It is so transparent, this interest of men—it feels sometimes like a heat-seeking missile. It then becomes a question of their intentions and how to react; a man on the subway, a week ago, insisted on sitting next to Tika as she came on the Red line from Emerson, and by the time they were crossing the Charles River he was handing her his card. He was older, in his forties, overweight and aggressive. They went underground again, and at the next stop she got up and walked out the doors and, in full view of the man, deposited his card into a Dumpster. She'd been furious that she'd had to get off at a stop she normally wouldn't depart at; furious that he'd altered her routine. But you could tell, with some men, that they wouldn't get the hint, even if you dropped word about your boyfriend, and sometimes you just didn't feel like laying down the law and asking them to leave you the hell alone. This man is no problem—he's just been caught staring—but she moves a little toward Jesse, and when she feels the man looking again, she turns her back on the stranger and engrosses herself in the magazine.

Tika flips open the pages of *Rolling Stone,* landing on a two-page spread for the movie *O,* with the faces of Mehki Phifer, Josh Hartnett, and Julia Stiles. *Trust. Seduction. Betrayal . . . Everything Comes Full Circle,* the ad promises. Tika imagines herself in the new, glitzy Loews Theatre near Emerson with Jesse, the two of them close in the steep darkness, having salty popcorn and Pepsis, the story unfolding before them. She looks up to tell Jesse that she wants to see the movie, sees he is engrossed in his magazine, and so does not disturb him.

She turns the page and finds Kascha, in an Armani Exchange ad, posing with a dark, Italian male model, the two of them caught as if on a forbidden date, the lights of a city blurred behind them. Kasha's hair is dyed to a dark shade and her bangs are cut to fall just over her eyebrows. Both models look at the camera warily, as if caught in an affair, in something illicit. "Hey," Tika says to Jesse, who is flipping pages again. "Here's sis. She told me she would be in the Armani this week."

Jesse leans over and smiles down at the photograph. He kisses her at the temple. "Pretty cool," he says, nodding. "I can't get over how strange it must be to see your sister in these things."

"It's usually pretty cool," Tika says quietly.

Sometimes it had been frightening in New York last year, though, during fashion week, seeing her sister on the catwalk, so famous now, in the center of all that, all of those eyes of yearning. Tika will be used to it this time—flashbulbs so intense that they seem to stop Kascha in time, to make even the live Kascha into a series of photographs. People stopping Kascha on the street, pressing in for autographs. Tika and Kascha will stay at the Barbizon, a great escape; in the room it will be as if they are teenagers again, and Tika will recover a part of herself. There will be the windows over glittering New York, and it will be as though she and her sister own the world.

She goes with Jesse to the Indian vendor, and they buy the magazines.

Later, in the 24/7 Burger Palace a few blocks down, earnest Jesse questions Tika. They sit close together in a booth, a hanging light above them, waiters and waitresses moving constantly by to the kitchen. Tika holds Jesse's hands, massages the heaviness of them with her fingers. Neil Diamond sings about being lost between two shores, and in Jesse's eyes is the light of concern for this intrusion into her world.

"She seems to be going to a lot of trouble," he says. "Why this Australian, Tike? Just for the thrill of it?"

"It's complicated with Susan," Tika says. She lays one hand over Jesse's fingers, uses the other to sip her lime rickey. The restaurant is crowded, a small ocean of conversations just beyond their island. A waitress slips their burgers and fries onto the table, and Jesse and Tika thank her, and Tika goes back to the massage; after gigs, Jesse is always grateful for the pressure on his fingers. Tika says,

"The truth is, like Jiri and Anna said, it shows me how I don't know her very well. I mean, I moved in and I didn't know her except through her ad. And Kascha was happy I was just living with somebody. And we've gotten along okay up to now. But I think I know what's happening. This is something some men are kind of thick about"—she smiles and runs the pad of her forefinger over Jesse's wrist—"present company excluded, of course. But you want to be with a guy who *understands* you, who lets you be who you are *unconditionally*. Women are always being contained or put on some pedestal and you want to be in a situation where you know you can mess up and still be accepted. Susan's mom is this uptight *bitch,* honest to God. So I'm doubting Susan gets any real understanding from her family. Her father is like, *long* gone, living in California, and she just talks to him sometimes long distance. I've met a couple of her sisters, and you can see that the mother is this incredible chore for them, too. I went to this concert at Jordan Hall last year? With Susan and her mom? And Evelyn was driving and we dropped Susan off to get the tickets, and I'm in the car with Evelyn and we pull into this handicapped space and Evelyn whips out this handicapped card and I guess she sees the way I'm looking because she says, 'They're easy to get.' She totally misunderstood my look. I mean, I dunno, maybe she is handicapped somehow, but I've never seen her have trouble walking or anything. And I was going to say something, but then I'm thinking, *This is Susan's* mom, *and maybe she's got some problem I shouldn't meddle into, maybe she is handicapped.* But it just seemed consciously *selfish* to me, you know? I asked Susan about it later and she said, 'Oh, *Mom,* man, she's got the system *rigged.*'"

Tika remembers Jordan Hall, the great egg shape of the place, the hush in musical silences, the "Hallelujah Chorus" being sung beneath them, and the opened choir books looking like a flock of birds wanting to fly. The thing with the handicapped space still bothering her. Evelyn Bristol's face intent, glasses on her nose, and Susan's profile looking already like her mother's.

"Evelyn's always asking Susan these questions, you know, 'Susan, do I look good in this blouse, should I get my lips Botoxed, should I lift my chin, should I have had sex with this guy on the first date?' Just like, this narcissist. Susan just laughs about it after and says her mom is so whacked, but I can tell it fucks her up. It seems to me some of this is stuff a mother should *never* be talking to her daughter about; then she mixes that with the normal criticism, you know, 'Susan, you ought to be more careful with your money; Susan, you look heavy in that color,' shit like this. I don't know what happened with Susan's dad but I can see why he didn't hang around."

Jesse nods thoughtfully, then disengages his hands, saying, "Thanks, Tike." He takes a bite of his burger. He's ordered the Macho Burger—it is the only thing he ever orders—and he can barely get his mouth around it. His eyes through the glasses, so busy concentrating on the burger, make Tika smile. When he's swallowed and brushed his lips with a napkin he says, "So you mean Susan feels like she has to go to extremes to find her own world, her own, what did you say? *Unconditional*—"

"Yeah, and probably she gets it, somehow, from Stuart. That's what Anna says."

"Well," Jesse says, dipping a fry into ketchup, "I'll guess he loves up a good *game,* Tike. Men are good at it. You act a little caring and get the girl in bed as long as you want, and then you say you need some space and go through like a week of her bitching at you and then it's freaking over. Some guys don't even bother listening to the bitching. And this guy's got it good. Because he can come here and have the sex whenever he wants and when it gets too heavy, *pow,* he just goes to Australia. And what can she do to him? Well, I guess she could call his wife?"

Tika considers. "A few days ago I would have said she wasn't capable of it, of breaking up a family. But she's doing it anyway, right? And like Anna told me, I'm realizing that I just don't know her. That's the saddest part of this. I had a friend, and now I don't know who the hell she is."

Jesse and Tika watch each other, holding their burgers. Neil Diamond is ending his song, *"leaving me lonely still . . . ,"* and Tika knows that Jesse is thinking about her own father, wondering what he can say.

"He was the most *romantic,*" Tika says, and her father is here with her, walking a cobblestoned street, ancient tenements of Rome behind him, a dry evening wind whisking his tie over his shoulder.

"Who?"

"My father. You were thinking about him."

"I was thinking about how close you were to him."

"Oh, we *were* close," Tika says. "You always felt closer to your*self* after being with him."

"I know what you mean," Jesse says. "Some people are like that. Some people you hang out with, and when you leave them, after being at a party or whatever—"

"You feel better about who *you* are. Because they care about being with you instead of showing off how great *they* are. Dad was just like that," Tika says. She is quiet a few moments as Jesse goes after his burger again; she remembers her father meeting her in Italy, bundling her into his arms. Happily buying her the Leica set in Rome, saying, *You will love the photography, it will help you see the world, honey*. Remembers him on the Spanish Steps and at the Fountain of the Naiads; mornings that autumn when he said a cheery, *Hello, pretty lady,* to the heavy woman who owned a market near their hotel and how the woman smiled and peered out at them from her doorway, vegetables and hams and sausage hanging from her walls with twine; the women vendors on that street joked and flirted shamelessly with Tika's father.

Her father: Jean-Louis LaFond. A former French tennis ace with a quick, warm smile. A rainy evening, looking from the Gardens of Lucullus over the Piazza del Popolo to St. Peter's Basilica, the wetness on the tar making lights glow, the dome against a pink and purple sky. October. The clean-shirt-cologne smell of him as Tika leaned against him, closed her eyes. Her father's lips on the crown of her head, his hand across her forehead. Now in her memory it is the September before Rome, when her father still lived at home, in Andover, in northern Massachusetts. *Around now, around this time in September,* she will tell Jesse. She will tell him now, and she will tell him again much later, in darkness, in more detail, after they have made love. *I looked down at the light with Kascha.* Tika was thirteen, Kascha sixteen; after school they had gone to the nearby lake on bicycles—swum to rafts that had not been taken in yet, up the ladder and dripping over those dry boards, adjusting bathing suits and then lying out on warm wood, watching the sun drift through clouds. Clouds darkening and a light rain starting, and they rode home, laughing, through increasing downpour. Then they showered, Tika after Kascha, and when Tika came out of the bathroom she expected to hear her father and mother downstairs, getting ready for dinner, but what she saw instead was her sister, in the darkened bedroom, at the window. Tika joined her there, looking through rain at the pool house where her parents were, the light blazing through the dark evening, white squares of evening grass, the pool a long, dark rectangle. The rain made a steady, hushing sound but Tika heard her mother's raised voice sometimes, a sound of betrayal, and in that sound Tika saw her father at the club where he taught most of his tennis lessons, that place that smelled so clean, outdoors and in, smiling at other, younger women. This had never surprised her, for she knew the way that women changed around her father; the way their voices grew light with him, as though they would never offer a burden to him with their presence. And she had seen her mother for years move away from her father's touches in the kitchen, sometimes brushing away his hands; it had always disturbed her. She saw her parents now walk across the window of the pool house, mostly her father in motion, his hands making gestures as if to the sky and then dropping to his sides in futility, their mother's voice, briefly rational, steeping into that sound of betrayal, and the circus of her father's arms would begin again, and her mother's voice would drop low, always putting in the last word.

Then her father stepped out into that straight rain. Not caring about it, raindrops drowning his khaki slacks and white shirt. That rain coming down as he walked to the driveway, to his car; once he looked up at the window and saw his daughters there. *What did we look like to him at that moment?* Tika wonders now, speaking into Jesse's eyes. *That last moment, my dad must have known, when we would be together on the same ground, in the same home.* For even if the bond between Tika's mother and father had been tenuous, and you'd had to force yourself to believe the circle was complete, they *had* been a family. Now that had been broken; they had ceased being a family a few minutes before, in the pool house, when something her mother said convinced her father that he'd had enough, his spirit could not live with her cloying coldness, a woman who wanted him to stay for appearances but who no longer wanted *him*. Tika thought that, on some level, her mother had still needed a certain intimacy, but it was some complicated, unstated intimacy that her father had no hope of creating for her. Maybe in the pool house her mother and father had simply formalized, or recognized, years of lying, of waking in the morning and going through the motions before the liberation of jobs: her mother driving to her job at the public relations firm in Newburyport, her father to the Andover Racquet Club—work neither had to do, for they had come from extremely well-to-do families.

"—he was looking up at us and his white shirt was all streaked and Kascha and I were crying," she says now. "And he could have been just going to town to get away from her for a while but we knew, and I could tell he was crying, too. Because he wanted to come up and tell us, like all the other times, that everything would be all right, that sometimes he and Mom just didn't get along. But he couldn't lie to us. And he put his head down and walked across to the car and for a moment I thought that he might be back soon, at least, but then Kascha and I just knew he wouldn't come back to the house and we couldn't even fucking *speak,* we started crying so hard. I mean, they both had affairs. But my mother—it was like she just lived in some other fucking *uni*verse when it came to emotions. I can remember how Kascha for a while started playing flute—she really got good at it—but if she picked it up to play anywhere around my mom, my mom just left the room—"

"Why? *Jesus,*" Jesse says.

"Because it was *emo*tional," Tika says. "Like anything *emo*tional she walked out on. She still does. Kascha took things like that hard.

She won't admit it, but she did. Who knows how it happens? I mean, my mother's parents were all right but *religious* as all get-out, and sometimes my grandmother could be a really cold fish. Shit like that just runs in families, that coldness just goes on and on until somebody stops it—"

Jesse is watching her; his family, blue-collar and close, from Haverhill, is a loving one, and he doesn't understand this. She watches him think about it. Then he says, "But your dad must have seen something in your mom, early on—"

"Oh yeah." Tika waves a French fry, dips it into ketchup, and takes a bite. "Oh, my mother was beautiful all right, and I'm sure she was warm once, before the marriage started going south. She's a good enough actress when she needs to be. And my dad was this handsome tennis professional who had competed at Wimbledon, and she could show him off to all of her society friends. And he tried a few businesses of his own and when they didn't work out I think my mother saw him as a failure. You could hear it in their conversations. Like she started talking down to him."

"And suddenly being the handsome tennis pro you could show off wasn't good enough."

"Exactly." Tika has a moment of remembering her father teaching her to serve when she was twelve, the easy toss, the smooth bend of body, his racket back and coming forward powerfully, and people above the court, pressed against glass, watching. There was the father-smell of the place, of newness, plastic and rubber, nylon netting, tennis balls, aluminum rackets, the sound of being within a huge funhouse cave.

"But after the split-up he went to France, and Kascha was already on her first modeling assignment in Milan, and Dad called her and she spent time with his family in Aix-en-Provence—they're really great people, I want you to meet them"—she imagines this, Jesse being hugged in the living room of the old stone château, seeing this warm part of her family—"and then he called me, and I was pretty angry, ending up in high school in Andover, my sister and my father gone, my sister having this glamorous life and my mother not wanting me to see my father. And my father called me up when he knew my mother would still be at work, and he said, 'Why don't you fly to Milan, and I'll pay for it, and we'll visit your sister and then the two of us can go to Rome? And you can tell your mother you've just gone to see your sister, if she has a problem with it.' Of course she had no problem with Dad paying the ticket. And I didn't tell her about seeing him. And Dad knew Rome really well and he took me everywhere. And he was so happy I was there; he'd just spent a week with Kascha, and he was really proud of her and her career, and I could feel he was proud of me, too, even though I hadn't done anything that year but flunked geometry and advanced biology *both*—"

"But you were his daughter. None of the rest of it mattered."

Tika nods, feels her eyes brimming. "Mostly, in Rome, we just talked. There are these steps near the Spanish embassy, and we would sit there for hours together talking, watching the world go by. Things were easy with Dad. He made you feel like anything was possible."

She wipes her cheekbone with the back of her hand, and Jesse takes the hand and kisses it. Billy Joel is singing about how it is such a lonely world, and Tika is imagining a week after she left Rome, her father driving in the Italian Alps. There was a woman with him. In newspaper accounts afterward the woman looked stunning, with long dark hair, demure eyes and lips—nothing like Tika's blond mother. Tika feels—she always does when she thinks of this—the highway blurred in front of the Citroën, clouds over the breathtaking valley. Then bikers there, by the side of the road, one of them falling and others swerving and her father swerving the car and another car rushing up around the curve and hitting the Citroën solidly in the back right side, sending it into a spin, and how it must have sounded when they went through the guardrail and the tires lost the ground and the car went into space: light, a moment of sun spinning above and the rushing in your ears, the screaming of the woman.

Tika stood there, at that curve in the mountains, a few days later, with Kascha, the two of them holding each other. The light was flat and together they'd watched the mountains, the valley.

Jesse is holding her hand tight against his forehead, his eyes closed, as if joined with her in prayer. Then he opens them and looks very directly at her. In Aix-en-Provence it was snowing, the flakes landing on the backs of her fingers as she touched the earth, her father's grave. Kascha beside her. Her French family, her mother, standing around the girls.

"Some cousin of my father's—she didn't know better, but you know the French, scared of silence, always creating conversation," Tika says, her throat tight, "said at the funeral reception to my mother, 'But isn't it fortunate that Jean-Louis could spend those last weeks with his daughters?' And my mother waited until we got on the plane before she went ballistic on me. It was so fucking bad that when we were flying over the sea I went to another part of the plane to sleep, just to get the hell away from her. Hell, Jess, I'm never going to live in fucking Andover again."

"It wasn't right of her," Jesse says, stroking her hand on the table. "Doing that after you just lost your father."

Tika is remembering. "It didn't seem to affect her much at all, his dying. She just seemed more angry at him. I don't know. Maybe she fucking cried at night when nobody was looking."

"It sounds like that is how she would handle it."

"One of the last things my dad told me," Tika says, "was, 'Your mother has a lot of sadness in her, and when she goes crazy just think of the sadness and let your anger go, if you can.' To tell you the truth, I was glad it came out that Kascha and I saw him, because it would have been hard for me to keep the lie going. I'm not very good at lying. Kascha was living in Italy, but I was seeing Mom every day."

"Jesus, Tika. I didn't know about this part of it, seeing your father and hiding it—"

"Yeah, well," Tika says, "like I was thinking at the show. We all have these ghosts, right?"

"At the show?"

"Elijah. The song you wrote with him."

"Oh." Jesse shakes his head. "Poor freaking Elijah. He says he wants to be a star so she'll see what she missed."

"Not a good reason to do it."

Jesse shrugs, smiles. "Makes him ambitious, anyway." He kisses her fingers. Elton John is starting into "I Guess That's Why They Call It the Blues." Jesse leaves bills under his glass, and the John song is still in Tika's head when they walk to the T. Fewer people are out now, the fire performers gone. The Coop clock stands at nearly midnight. The night is exquisite, cool, and some of the kids by the subway, dressed in their baggy prison pants, are kicking around a beanbag, trying to keep it in the air. Down below, the air of the subway is warm and as they wait Tika leans back against Jesse's chest and then the train is a red, howling rectangle; it slows and stops, and the doors open with a hiss and they step in and soon they are rolling beneath the Charles River, into the city.

NINE

Ghost-Man hears the Elton John song as he turns, ten paces behind Alison Tiner, into the grocery aisle. She bypasses the wines, for she has a well-stocked wine rack at home, in her pantry. Her bottles there are dusty, so Ghost-Man has not attempted to take them out to memorize them, imagining obvious streaks of his cloth-glove fingers on the glass, or worse, one of the bottles slipping from his hand, shattering on the floor—that would be all he'd fucking need. So he's read what he could of the bottles as they sat, where the natural kitchen light falls over them at an angle: *Wild Vines Blackberry Merlot* and *Sutter Home* and *Robert Mondavi* whites and *Bella Sera Pinot Grigio*. He passes some of these now with his cart, bright vanilla colors, deep reds.

In the water and soda aisle Ghost-Man grasps a six-pack of Poland Spring, tears one of these off, twists off the cap, takes a meth from his pocket and swallows it down with the water. Soon he will feel the almost unbearable soaring, and that thing that the rice has done to his insides will be in retreat. At the end of the aisle, Alison Tiner is considering premade sauces for the chicken.

Her man has been coming less frequently of late to visit, and Ghost-Man has seen her shadow pace across the curtain often after their phone calls. This all followed a time when Alison Tiner was gone for a few days (Ghost-Man had been afforded a chance to inspect her apartment closely then); presumably she had decided to stay *on top* of her lover, to spend whole days with him, as a woman will at an early point in a relationship, and then will realize that her boyfriend is being polite but badly needs some time away from her, some space. *How coquettish you have become since, dear Alison,* Ghost-Man thinks. *Now your phone calls are receptive, rather than assertive. How clever of you!*

Alison Tiner glides along with her cart, not nodding at all to the many shoppers who pass her, her head cocked at that odd angle. Ghost-Man knows she is planning. Putting together provincial female plans to draw her man back in: food, sex. He wants to tell her that she needs to exercise some intelligence here and not simply mold herself about the desires of her lover! *The world changes according to what you do, Alison! When you decide—when you even breathe! You affect everything!* He imagines Alison Tiner's dirty feet in the air, jerking slightly with the thrusts of her boyfriend, the male ass clenching, her body molding around his penetration.

He follows her past the breads, the bakery, the small in-store bank; she goes to the register, speaking only a few words to the cashier, runs her credit card through, and takes her receipt and groceries. In Ghost-Man's chute next to her Kascha LaFond stares from a magazine rack—shining lips, eyes of anticipation.

Alison Tiner walks from the store, the small bag in the crook of her left arm, her hair slightly askew, tied at the back of her head, her head cocked a little up and to the left, working her hips, utilitarian. Ghost-Man pays for his groceries, watching her disappear into the glossy window, and puts his cardboard package in the paper bag, slipping it beside the chili and soy milk, and then he is on the sidewalk of Kirkland and out of the bright lights of the store and beneath trees he sees Alison Tiner walking, looking into windows, a small grocery, a Laundromat just closing for the night, a darkened insurance office. She slows, attracted by something in the window of a closed travel agency: Ghost-Man is sailing already, euphoric, and his anger seems to be slipping into his shirt, into the stitching of it—it might be a fluid that escapes his body and hides in this cloth construction. In this lightness he can almost forgive Alison Tiner her stupidity. His knees, his stomach, his shoulders, could lift off the ground altogether, carry him to the height of the trees, where he might look down on the woman staring into the travel office with her longing, might even feel sorry for her in her desperation.

She stares at a poster advertising Rio. Ghost-Man stops a few feet from her, looking at a travel poster himself, feels her glance at him, at his bag of groceries, decide he is not dangerous, go on reading. Ghost-Man gazes at a poster of Greece: white homes on an island, a dark blue sea. He sneaks a look over at Brazil, at Alison Tiner imagining herself there with her man. Ghost-Man wants to tell her that he was on his honeymoon there. He thinks of his wedding to Jenna in Maine, a piano playing, a floor of beautiful hardwood, women whispering to their partners as they danced, their dresses flowing. Large windows of the old inn looking out onto the rocky seacoast. Then the lights of Rio beneath their plane, Jenna asleep on his shoulder. *Do you know,* he wants to ask this woman (who with her cock of head seems to offer the sense that she knows everything) *that on the Brazilian statues of Christ they never hide the whip marks? They tell the* truth. *They show the streaks of* blood, *the fucking* agony. *They don't sanitize this shit the way we do. Americans in their fear of death sanitize* everything, *even* the blood of the Messiah.

It is hard to concentrate for a moment. He might rise into the trees, his thighs feel so incredibly light. What a moment! He might tell Alison Tiner the truth about Christ! He might do it. In this next moment, or this next. He holds his bag close, feeling his heart beat against it, listens to Alison Tiner breathe.

TEN

Jiri is with Helena in the garden, towering heads of sunflowers over them, sunlight on cabbage leaves, smells of oregano, scallions, basil. His sister walks out through the break in the wall and Jiri follows, toddling on the path to the Horák hill, imitating Helena's fingers as she picks blackberries there. *See, taste,* she says, and the blackberries fall apart easily, tart in his mouth. There is the thick smell of wild grass and trees, the smell of Bohemia, and when she moves the sunlight seems to whiten her face above him.

But now he is an old man on Trowbridge Street again and the memory book is open on the table. There is sweat at his cheeks, and under his T-shirt. He has written two and a half pages of Czech and English and some German; sometimes just a few words represent whole thoughts—the writing abandoned when he got lost in memory. These sections are frustrating to read over, but rather than correct them he presses on. Near the window a crow is cawing, an ancient assault on the night. Dark leaves brush against the screen.

Jiri blinks. His lover Alena is somewhere in his memory, too, and he remembers that he wanted to say more about her. He can hear the sounds of insects and a car door, perhaps on Irving Street, slamming. The garage roof is below him, and his brow creases at what he is unable to do. He closes his eyes and concentrates, then opens them again to the light. He takes one of Marjorie's fresh sheets. He writes in Marjorie's ovals first:

Who: Alena
What: stopping the train
Where: in the forest outside Plzeň
When: 1943

Start with a sound, he thinks—Marjorie Legnini often emphasizes this—*of kestrels in trees.* It is November, sky gray, very late afternoon. The birds call and slip from tree to tree above him. Jiri lies on the forest floor, his submachine gun beside him, looks down through branches at the railroad, black-and-silver rails. There are more trees on the opposite side of the tracks, and then the trees clear and there is a stretch of wild grass on both sides, bled nearly white by cool autumn, and about two hundred meters away an abandoned warehouse and, distantly, a steel bridge and warped loading dock, and the tracks curling south. The sun above is a flat white coin behind clouds.

On the train that is coming, according to Resistance members working with Czechoslovak Railways, there is a physicist named Jedlička, formerly of the Prague Technical University, who must be taken alive, along with his wife and as many Jews as they can save; Jedlička and the other Jews shall arrive in a single cattle car, eighty strong, at the end of a string of twelve freight cars that will be carrying munitions from the Škoda Works (these must be blown, quickly, with plastic explosives) and supplies for the Russian front. There will be extra guards on the train; they will be killed or incapacitated. This, along with getting to and opening the car with the Jews, is Jiri's job. Jiri checks his watch: twenty-three minutes left.

Four other Resistance men lie beside him, along with Alena and Hana Krásová, a Jewish woman in her forties who has joined them recently. There are another eight Resistance members directly opposite, on the other side of the tracks, hidden well behind large stones and brush. The forest floor is cold and you can feel the early breath of winter coming from it.

Now, from behind the abandoned warehouse, three men, headed by the figure of Dr. Kobera, jog quickly down the opposite side of the tracks. The men bend over the rails and organize sticks of dynamite there, where the rails are curving, and then run back toward the warehouse, their heads down, crouching, and they are gone behind the wall and corrugated tin roof and Jiri ducks and there is a massive *crack* splitting the air, cinder and wood debris settling like a harsh shower of rain, and when he looks up some of the debris is still floating over the milky sun. Jiri brings the submachine gun close to him; it smells of oil. He has three of these German egg grenades, also, hanging over his shoulder, resting on the ground now between him and a man in his thirties named Mulák. Jiri glances out at the fresh destruction on the tracks, a rail twisting savagely away from the smooth curve, two of the ties upended; one of the men—it looks from here like Štěpán Petřík—has run out and is kicking the ties, to no avail, to at least lay them flat, and the other two men run out and try to help, but the upended wood is stubborn and they give it up and jog again behind the warehouse.

They wait now. Jiri thinks of Alena and how she rocked him, how she still seems to be rocking him, her long legs curling over his back, her lips kissing his throat. He wonders if she is thinking of him. He cannot see her face past the heavy, unshaven face of Mulák, but he sees the curve of her shoulder, her hair tied back beneath a scarf. They might die here, he and Alena and the others—there are not many of them, perhaps not enough. It moves through him coldly, this possibility of death. Well, he does not want to see Alena die, but what of it for him? What better way for him to die? Alena's father, from Cheb, an anti-Nazi professor before the war, was shot right in front of her. She told him about it last night, after lovemaking, how the Nazi officer held the gun to her father's head and fired and her father fell to the ground and she and her mother screamed in horror and the Nazi walked away, bored with their hysterics. *You come to a point where you just want a small measure of justice,* Alena said, her chin jutting out a moment. *Just to kill as many of them as I can. That's all I want in life. I'm not asking for anything else.*

That's what I want, Jiri said.

The train comes, a small sound at first. Jiri hears it but cannot see it, and then, glancing carefully over Mulák's and Alena's heads, he sees the black rectangle of it, through the rusting structure of the bridge, the triangle of headlights. Steam running up and back, a black iron block growing into the turn with the flatbeds, the shapes of tanks and guns beneath tarpaulins, freight cars behind, now coming beneath the bridge and larger, so you feel it in the ground. Then the shrieking lock of metal on metal—it goes on forever, this howling, you cannot think in its loudness—and the black rectangle tilts suddenly, burrowing into the cinders, thundering by them, and Jiri is getting up, watches the long train sliding, slowing, dust rising into the flat sky. Frantic German is snapping in the air and there is female screaming, faintly, and Jiri is scrambling down the embankment with the others, hearing submachine-gun fire from the opposite side of the train, a metallic thumping like the sound of clubs against a metal door. Mulák and Alena are beside him, and Hana and the others are already firing ahead, and there is fear in Jiri's thighs and throat, but he tells himself, *Screw this fear. I don't mind dying killing these sons of bitches.* He clears the trees and brush, and there is a small dip before the railroad bed, and then he feels the rise in his legs and the Nazi guards are dropping above from the sides of the train. Mulák and Alena and Jiri fire, a furious, quick exchange of bullets, and suddenly Mulák is falling and Jiri turns and sees him, on the ground, his forehead disintegrated into flesh and red and Jiri is ducking, running on the cinders now in the shadows of the train beside him, and there is a snapping of a 9 mm bullet passing him, and another, and other gunfire near him, the metallic knocking. When a gray uniform steps down five meters in front of him, black pin of gun aiming, Jiri does not wait but fires, the submachine gun tight to his chest, jumping, and the guard turns halfway and drops from Jiri's bullet, and a moment later Jiri is leaping over the body, a quick impression of the German face sideways, blood running from mouth, dark on cinders, gravel. He shoots ahead madly, takes part of the face of another guard, who stumbles into brush at the bottom of the railroad bed. Jiri fires after him, bullets thumping into body. There is the smell of cordite, a sweet smell of blood.

Jiri and the others come to the last car, and still there is a gun battle behind him, the explosion of a grenade on the other side of the train. He grabs a rusting handle to the car and slides the door open—so many faces, dirty, people packed tightly, exclaiming, baffled at the sudden light, harsh, immediate smells of urine and vomit. Some of the Jews have died from suffocation and are corpses, standing up, and there is wailing as these dead are discovered, and the Resistance people, coming in now from the fighting, are saying, *Quickly, we must move quickly,* and Jiri sees Dr. Kobera watching those coming off the train sharply, saying then, *Dr. Jedlička; your wife? With me, please, sir.* A balding man, disoriented, a heavyset woman. Alena, on the other side of the door from Jiri, is helping down an old woman and saying, *Neděleite si starosti. Mother, it will be all right.*

The dead are passed to the door, and Jiri, helping to carry off a dead teenage girl, trying not to look at her white face, her opened mouth and dull teeth, is suddenly transfixed by a bracelet on her wrist. It is almost like the one he bought for Helena: golden varnished wood, a pattern of intricate flowers and greens. Perhaps even purchased at the same shop in Plzeň. He tightens his jaw, carries the corpse, lays her a few feet from the cinders beside other bodies, and here is her mother, who had apparently not understood in the shock of the journey that her daughter had died; the mother kneeling, a god-awful sudden keening that is cut off by others who cover her mouth and weep with her. They cannot hold her, and she stumbles forward and embraces her daughter, trying to get the girl up, off the ground. Jiri stares at the bracelet, the daughter's face in death; at the gray roots of the mother's hair, the gray of her arms and neck, her face buried in her daughter's skin. He thinks desperately of the caves near Chrást that they must bring this mother and the others to, a forty-five-minute hike; the Nazi police are already well on the way. He pulls the mother gently from behind. *We must go, Mother,* he says.

Já ji nemůžu nechat—

My musíme jit. We must go.

Writing at this kitchen table fifty-eight years later, Jiri is stunned at how immediate everything is when his pen is on the page, at how the writing has led him to the mother and daughter, the bracelet. The struggle of the mother's flesh and muscle, how she begged to stay and die with her daughter, and how Alena and Štěpán had to help Jiri bring her into the forest. She took the bracelet with her, walked with it clutched to her chest, rocking, tears streaming from her eyes. The mother had hardly flinched as the train was blown behind her, as the others turned back with the concussions, orange light on their faces. She kept staring forward in shock. Jiri walked beside her, stepping quickly; he and Alena and Štěpán and a small group of twenty made their way quietly through the trees. Jiri kept his hand on the mother's arm the whole way. He turned to her and watched that last light of dusk on her face, then the darkness, her face quivering, looking down, her eyes filling in disbelief. She said, *Ja ji nemuzu nechat? What will they do with my baby? She is all alone there,* and Jiri said, *But her spirit is not there anymore, Mother. They can do nothing to her. She is with us now. We must keep moving. Keep moving with me, just stay with me.*

III

ELEVEN

Who: Mother
What: the day after Heydrich died—coming home with birthday material from Šaškova's
Where: Lidice, home
When: June 1942

Jana is grateful this morning to bump into Lidice with Petr Jaroš, her brother-in-law, to wake in his Škoda car, her canvas satchel on the seat beside her. Petr nods and smiles a little as she comes out of an anxious sleep. She was shopping for fabric in Prague yesterday with her sister, Sophie (the blue print material for Helena's birthday dress is in the satchel now, from Šaškova's on Bethlehem Square, and Jana can finally go to work on it), then visiting the relatives, delivering the small paintings by Helena and Jiri. At the old homestead in Plzeň last night, where Sophie and Petr now live, there was the news on the radio of Heydrich's death. A terror had run quickly through Jana; she'd said, *I must get to my family.* But, of course, travel in darkness—with headlights—was completely out of the question. *All will be well,* Petr had said, trying to reassure her, *if we make no motion to attract the beasts.* So Jana lay awake much of the night, in her childhood room, full of worry for her family.

Here are the familiar walls and tight buildings, the hardware store where Helena is working, the post office. St. Martin's Church glances by beneath the arc of sun. Atop the roof is Emile Hojda, a silhouette against the sky, crouched to his shingles. He has volunteered to make the repairs to the roof; the church is paying only for his materials. His three sons, Jana can see, are higher up, swinging hammers. Jana imagines what Emile Hodja sees: He is very high, for St. Martin's Church is built onto a hill. There will be a patchwork of the many red-tiled roofs and stove-top chimneys, small gardens behind each house just emerging from shadows, fields of green and gold where workers are already bundling hay, and the distant tree line and řepka fields. Emile Hodja's vision is the dream of a home she had with Ríša, so many years ago in Prague; they were students at Charles University, full of plans (he would be a science teacher, and she would have a small business doing upholstery to help their income, as she'd done with her mother). On and on Jana and Ríša had talked, their shadows slipping before them over Prague cobblestones.

They drive by the bus station—two Nazi soldiers sit in the shade there, crutches on the bench beside them; one is missing a leg. The other has the Lidice paper in his hands: Jana makes out the name *Heydrich* in the headline, a brief image of the SS general's thin, strange face. It took him seven days to die after the Resistance threw a grenade at his car, suffering he certainly deserved after the thousands he murdered in Czechoslovakia. But now the Nazis will be even more vicious, and there will be no more visiting of relatives, no going to Prague, for a long time to come. A fear is in her for her relatives, for her sister and happy, unshaven Petr—here he is, physically, beside her, talking and shifting gears, and with only a slight turn of events he might be gone; such is life now with these rulers.

The Škoda motors up Andělu and Petr drops Jana at her front door, apologizing that he cannot come in: He will be late for his shift at the Škoda factory and it is too dangerous now to raise any alarms. She says of course, kisses his rough cheeks, hugs him, takes her satchel. She waves as her brother-in-law swings in a circle and goes back down the hill.

A rabbit hangs on Jana's back doorknob, a deadweight in a small white burlap bag—she organized with Libor Čermák, the village butcher, to kill her animal just before she arrived home—and she puts the rabbit in the kitchen pantry and takes the canvas satchel to her bedroom. She eases the tissue-wrapped fabric for Helena's dress out of the satchel and puts it into a drawer, beneath a sweater of hers. She changes into a housedress and, in her kitchen, puts on an apron for chores.

In the late afternoon Jana cleans the rabbit and dices the meat, and leaves it a moment on the wooden chopping block; in the shadowed laundry house of the garden she takes an onion and potatoes from a hinged storage box and puts them in her apron. There is a section of the building they reserve for coal, and here she shovels a small tin bucket full and walks back through the sun. Young sunflowers bow their heads to her as if in greeting, and she smells the sunlight on the earth. She shovels the coal into her iron kitchen stove and lights it; she washes her hands and takes sunflower oil from the pantry, puts a bit on an iron pan, slides the meat into it, and cooks the rabbit, and the smell is so provocative that she swoons and must check the impulse to have some. While it browns she cuts the onion at the window, her eyes glassy, and sometimes her eyelids are forced closed; she steps away and watches over the young garden and the broken spot of wall where Jiri always reads in the last of the sunlight. Beyond it is the Horák farm, the red pitch of roof, the top of the gray mortar walls. Emile Hodja has recently done repairs there, too; she remembers the comfort of seeing the roofer there in the mornings, how when she did not feel like doing her chores she watched his industry for inspiration. He is a hard worker, Emile Hodja. When he is not fixing roofs, he is repairing clocks—last year, as another charity to the church, he fixed the broken clock of St. Martin's, and Jana thinks of this each time she hears the bells chime.

Blinking, she sweeps up the cut onions with a wide knife and, in three trips and without spilling, puts them into the sizzling skillet, waiting as they turn to glass.

The illegal birthday dance she had planned for Helena (it was to take place at Věra's Kafková's home next door, for Věra and her husband, Vladná, own a phonograph—an afternoon dance and dinner with the heavy curtains to the living room pulled and Vladná and Říša watching out for soldiers coming up Andělu, and Glenn Miller and Duke Ellington playing softly) is unquestionably off, but she can still have the dinner for her daughter here at the house. The Nazis don't allow the dancing, and one cannot tempt fate now, but a celebratory dinner—there is no law against that. She will have a few of Helena's closest friends here, and she can invite the boy her daughter seems to like—his name is Rudolf Hejma—if he and his family check out. She will ask Věra about them. Jana wanted to watch her daughter dance. She thinks of Helena in candlelight, grasping the hand and shoulder of the boy, the two of them beginning to move gracefully, and shakes her head angrily and swallows down her emotion and turns to the rabbit.

The crowns she will spend for the birthday pork (Libor Čermák will give it to her at a good price, under the table), the rationed coupons she will use for the dinner, will still require considerable sacrifice. But Jana has four rabbits living—she can hear them snuffling now, through the kitchen window—and there are three geese. This should help bring her family into mid-August; she might even be able to stretch her meat sources into September.

The rabbit is cooked. She covers it and sets it to the cooler side of the stove. She walks down the short hallway, into the bathroom, and, after putting towels beneath her knees, scrubs the steel bathtub of the fine coal dust that Jiri couldn't entirely get out last night, a constant, thankless job that they all participate in, for the men with their coal dust blacken it every day except Sunday. She scrubs the tiled floor then, the sunlight coming in over her, over the tub. Then she runs the water and bathes, a small luxury in this day. The floating of her back in the warm water loosens her muscles, seems to slightly separate the vertebrae of her spine. She washes and rises and dries her body and then feels guilty for lying in comfort on the bed in her and Říša's bedroom, when the rest of the family is working, but tells herself she will be no good to anyone tired into her bones or sick. In the drawer beside her she puts her watch, lays it next to the oval wooden container with Jiri's gift. Jana thinks of the bracelet on Helena's wrist, just before she sleeps. She told Jiri how beautiful it was; she told him of her plans to make the dress. She thinks of the dress, finished, on her daughter—tiny yellow and red flowers against blue, like hope, like something you might paint on an egg at Easter.

Then in her dream SS General Reinhardt Heydrich is in the doorway, looking at her, and she wakes with a start, her heart hammering.

Helena is home. Jana hears her in the kitchen; she rises and goes to her daughter and kisses her cheeks and hugs her, and Helena says, "We are fine, Mother, but we were worried about you."

Helena goes back to grating the potatoes for dumplings. Jana gets a bowl, salt, egg, and flour, moving into this dance the two of them participate in. Říša and Jiri have arrived, too, banging their coal-stiffened clothes against the garden wall, hanging them over a line there in the corner, and then Jiri comes in to bathe and kisses Jana's cheek quickly, and she brushes back his hair and touches his face, feeling swelling there, at the cheekbone and eye, and he says, quickly "Dobrý den, Mother." And she says "Jiri," thinking, *Did a Nazi do this?* It swoops through her stomach, but she does not say more; Jiri walks directly into the bathroom and she can feel that he is upset, worked up, and the bathtub water is running; she steps out into the garden where Říša stands, philosophically, in his shorts, looking down on the Horák farm, the fields of grain, and beyond at the golden řepka in the hills.

Říša turns to her as she approaches; there are infinitesimal wood chips in her husband's hair, in his ears, in his eyebrows. She holds him a moment: her thinning Říša. Kisses his cheek. The hands she takes, kneading the swell of thumbs, are callused, with dried blood on the knuckles. The forearms are muscular and with fresh cuts. She turns them over, looks at them, looks at Říša's eyes. Helena, through the window, is boiling salted water and on the counter next to the stove mixing up the dumplings in a bowl.

"*Co se mu stlo?*" Jana says. "He is not himself."

"There was a fight, at lunch," Říša says.

"Jiri was in the fight?" Jana says, feeling her mouth go dry.

"Even *I* was in it," Říša says, smiling and gesturing at his hands, "though I'm afraid I didn't give much of an account of myself—"

"Well, what was it?"

"Communists. Always Communists. On the coal trucks. They don't think like Czechs anymore. They just think like Moscow. First defending Hitler—now after Heydrich dies saying Stalin will save us! Such goddamn fools." Říša shakes his head.

"It is amazing they didn't turn on Stalin when he got in bed with Hitler," Jana says. "They are as stupid as Stalin is horrible."

"They were telling us—Jiri, and me, and Smetáček and Rejsek—you know him, from Kladno?—that Stalin would save us all! Can you believe? And Jiri told them, and he is right, that Stalin will just rape the country the same way Hitler has and one of them came at Jiri—"

Jana imagines the fistfight as Říša tells it: Říša jumping in immediately to defend his boy and the others, too, hitting suddenly, getting swept up in it, the sound of guttural male fury. Czech guards coming and hitting with clubs and telling everyone they were fools, to shut up. The few Nazi guards looking on, watching to see if something should be done, if someone should be shot to take the starch out of the others.

"You cannot *do* this," Jana says in horror. "*Říša.* The fighting will just get someone killed."

"*Ano.*" Říša is nodding. Jana knows he tried to calm down his hotheaded teenage son. Knows that Říša has reproached himself all afternoon for failing. "You're right, *drahoušku*. We cannot let these things happen. We must somehow ignore the philosophies of these idiots or just tell them right away to shut up, before it gets out of hand. I told Jiri all of it after. But I must say"—Říša leans to Jana and lowers his voice—"our son fights like a lion. And Rejsek told me Jiri made a point of matching the Communists shovel for shovel all afternoon."

Jana sees it: her son with the black and wooden shovel swinging and the sun overhead. The sky like bright tin. Jiri's teeth gritted against the strain. She feels pride, fear, sorrow, fluttering in her. "You cannot do this, Říša," she says. "You cannot let it happen."

At dinner, with candles lit, Jiri volunteers nothing, much as Helena tries to lecture him about getting into fights.

Říša clears his throat. "And how was Prague?" he asks his wife.

She fills them in on the relatives: She and Sophie visited old aunt Milena Posseltová, on Vinohradská, and later had lunch with Uncle Aleš and Daniela Jarošová at their flat on Bethlehem Square.

"They all send greetings. But it is strange now, everyone afraid," Jana says. "Many of the shops are closed. There are SS walking everywhere. And you cannot believe—on the Old Town Square they have put up this banner of Hitler—just before Týn Church. It is four or five stories tall, just his face. His *eyes* look so troubled—"

"A banner?" Jiri says.

"Like a square sail, this huge, heavy cloth. Held up with metal poles and wires," Jana says. "It is just his face—I don't know what it is for—and the swastikas are everywhere around, hanging from the building eaves. There was a stage in front of the banner, too, just built. It is like they are preparing for some gathering."

"Maybe something to do with the Heydrich," Helena says.

"It might be," Jana says. Jiri listens with his face lowered, his jaw working. Jana cannot tell what he is thinking, for his hair hangs a little over his eyes.

"Hitler like God," Říša says with disgust. "It means that nothing is important but Hitler."

"They are quite crazy," Helena says. "Two Wehrmacht came in during the morning today to buy sheets of plywood. They said they were repairing the Sokolovna ceiling. One of them couldn't stop giggling," she says. "It was like he had no control of himself. His companion kept apologizing for him."

"Were you frightened of them?" Jana asks.

"No, Mother. They've been in a number of times before. I just try to not react and I am polite and otherwise I ignore them."

"Quite right," Jana says.

Usually, after he makes his bed on the couch for sleep, Jiri will just tolerate his mother's hugging him, but tonight he puts his arms around Jana first and wishes her a good night; her boy, gangly and strong, is not a child anymore. She holds back, tightly, before he can break the connection.

The dark secrets of this day settle like the blackbirds at the edges of the fields. Jana dreams of the giant troubled eyes of the Führer, the angry face staring at Prague. Then of Heydrich: Moonlight comes from Andělu Street onto the bed and the dresser, falls over pictures of her family. There is the sound of cicadas through the window. Somewhere in the night a protective bird sings, and the grandfather clock in the living room strikes the half hour; there is a distant, heavy sound of drums. And there in the bedroom doorway stands the Reichsprotektor, tall, and in his full black Nazi regalia, death's head adorning his cap, SS leaves at his collar, his odd hips and thighs that seem those of a woman.

Jana cannot see the features of Heydrich's face, for it is in shadow, and she wakes with a frightful start and Říša beside her is in an exhausted sleep—his cheekbone an emaciated 7 in the pale light—and their room is exactly as it was in the dream, so that it is possible for Jana to believe that maybe the ghost of Heydrich is here, only now invisible.

She senses that a demon has come to threaten her family. She rises and steps across the cool tiled floor and stands there in the doorway, gooseflesh on her arms where her nightshirt falls away, gooseflesh on her neck; her hands rise, grip the doorframe. She stays there and slowly the room is more calm, her husband's intelligent features against the pillow. She goes back to the side of the bed and puts on her leather shoes and taps down the hallway and looks in on Helena in her very small room across from the bath; Helena's hair drifts over her eyes, and moonlight makes a triangle above her on the wall. Jana moves on to Jiri on the living room couch; his face, too, is exhausted, and bruised from the fight. The Philips radio is beside his head. Her son breathes deeply there, in the night. She wants to touch Jiri's face but is afraid to wake him and afraid that he would open his eyes to her weeping over his bruising, his young whiskers. The moonlight stretches over pictures on the stone mantel of Jiri with his Sokol group, standing on a field in Plzeň with their wooden rifles at age ten, and on a field trip to Prague, to the Old Town Square. And what is on those

Prague cobblestones now, before the church of Týn—the same place where her boy, with his buddies here, has stood? The same place where Kafka wove his stories, where Hus and Mozart and Copernicus walked? Now the portrait of insane Hitler, there for his insane followers to draw inspiration from. The Nazis are poisoning the nation. They do not believe that Czechoslovakia exists. *That my family exists.* Jana leans forward and kisses her boy and smells his hair and skin, and he stirs slightly in his sleep. And then she goes back over her solid, smooth wooden floor to her bed.

In the morning Jiri insists on taking a photograph of Jana and Helena as Helena prepares to go off to work. They pose leaning against Helena's bicycle, and Jana says, "For heaven's sake, hurry it up, Jiri, she can't be late."

Jiri tells them both to smile, and Helena laughs at the combination of her mother's impatience and Jiri's cheerfulness, and Jana cannot help laughing with her.

"I mean it, Jiri," she says, trying to recover, shaking her finger at him. "You need to take the picture and stop kidding about." She puts her arm around Helena, and then it is done and Helena is gliding down the hill, waving at the corner, and Jiri slips the film roll in his coat and ducks back into the house with his mother clucking after him.

When Říša and Jiri have gone, Jana sequesters herself in Věra Kafková's sewing room, by a second-floor window that looks down on her own garden. Věra's Singer is a more recent model than Jana's, and, since Jana often uses Věra's machine for more complicated projects, Helena will not think it unusual that her mother is doing work here. The plum trees that Jana shares with Věra are bright green through the window, shifting a little with wind—they seem, for a moment, almost to glitter. Jana starts cutting, the scissors making a decisive part through the tissue of her pattern and the cloth for the birthday dress—quick slashes: now the divided fronts, now the collars and sleeves, now the back. She has fashioned her pattern after a dress worn by Carole Lombard in *My Man Godfrey,* just before the war; Helena has talked of her favorite actress's style ever since seeing the film in Prague. It will have long cuffed sleeves and an offset neckline bow of white crinoline; one day, when the barbarians have gone, her daughter shall dance in it.

Jana works over the next two days whenever she can, the Singer needle diving steadily through Helena's dress and her projects for the Krušinas: an old canvas coat needing mending, curtains with plain casings for the Krušina kitchen, pillow covers for little Marta Krušinová's bedroom, two of Marta's dresses needing minor repairs. Sometimes Věra comes in, nodding with approval at the progress of the birthday dress. She brings Jana drinks of water and once a vase of wood sorrel and star flower, picked here on the Horák hill. Jana says, "*Děkuji,* Věra, they look wonderful," and watches her friend bend to a small table and put down the flowers, a new shadow on the floor.

Věra says, "Keep working, it looks very good—I shall make us something to eat whenever you are hungry," and then is gone, descending the stairs.

There is the pulsing sound of the cicadas, and as Jana sews she glances out the window and sees the hill falling away to the Horák farm, rows of young crops, grain, and the hills rise again to the forest. Some two miles in the distance there is the Krušina farm, and for a moment Jana would like her family to live there, with its availability of food, with its distance from the Nazis billeted here. The church bell sounds the hours, and Jana listens; she imagines others in her community looking up to the sound as well—it is part of their *history* that Emile Hodja has mended. It means nothing to the Nazis but hours marked. Below, the sunflowers are quiet now, the crickets sing, and the plum trees are heavy with their leaves.

On the next evening, a little after ten P.M., Jana paces with concern for her boy. It is still early yet for Jiri to be back from the Krušina farm, but she shall stay awake until he comes home, will give him something to eat, some potato pancakes and bacon when he returns. She steps out into the garden, listens to the crickets and frogs in the fields. The plum trees glow with their dark thickness, and the sunflowers suddenly have grown considerably, nodding at their moorings. The wall, the shed, her small garden, all are heavy with dew, and you can smell that wetness and the greenery. Jana thinks of collecting flowers in the morning with Věra—perhaps there will be time before rain comes—wood sorrel and black mustard and wolfbane, arranging them into vases, this freshness and life in the rooms of their families. She walks to the wall, clutching her robe tight to her. In the plum trees icterus birds are making brief, golden flights; she listens to them, watches them, waiting for her son, until another sound—an odd, heavy disturbance of truck engines—takes her suddenly from her thoughts.

The icterus birds scatter in a bright explosion.

TWELVE

The soldiers were everywhere, Věra Kafková told Jiri, on their night in Prague after the war. Motioning with her hands. *Everywhere. Like a swarm. They stayed outside the houses through the night and we watched them from the windows. Then in the early morning they came for the men and tore our homes apart and marched the women and children to the school.* Here Věra broke down, waving a hand at the futility of her emotions. *To bylo hrocné, honey. It was terrible.*

In his kitchen, Jiri has been writing it all down. He thinks he has his mother's face right: high cheekbones, skin Bohemian dark with sun, eyes the color of wheat. His mother's face—turning at the sound of the trucks, looking over the garden wall at the Germans coming down the Horák drive, hearing them on the streets. Then the violence: houses searched, everything thrown out windows, smashed. Jiri imagines the dress for Helena thrown into the garden dirt, the telescope he used with his father in pieces. He remembers how he sensed rather than saw Helena sleeping on that last night: his sister, a curving moment of white blanket, the shy triangle of light on the wall above her. His parents nodding to him in the shadows of the hallway and, when he looked back at the break in the garden wall, before going down the path, he saw his mother watching him from the back doorway, waving. Lidice under the moon as he slipped from town, up around the hayfields and the village below then to his right as he climbed up Liska hill toward the forest. Not a light to be seen in town, the stars over the dark shapes of houses and Fanta pond.

The night is quiet outside the screen window now: the garage where Jiri's Buick sits, the fence, a house beyond. A moth insists at the window, trying indefatigably for Jiri's light, bringing him from that last night in Lidice. Jiri thinks about driving with Tika in his car, *him* driving, to the Arboretum or to the sea, his eyes just a little better than they are now, and Tika saying, *It is amazing, Jiri, so wonderful, your recovery.*

A car goes by on Irving Street, through houses and trees, playing this rap, this heavy declaration of war, of angry existence. The rap music fades; in the relative quiet afterward the kitchen clock is synchronized with the grandfather clock in the living room. It is twelve-fifty. Jiri remembers the St. Martin's clock that Emile Hodja fixed, the simple, clear sound of it. He remembers three years later, in Prague—the Town Hall clock cracked by a Nazi missile. He was there, fighting with partisans in the uprising at the end of the war. He was running through the Old Town Square and there was the astronomical clock, split in half after four hundred years of operating, slumped in defeat; the Nazis were targeting historic artifacts. The clock had been so much a part of Jiri's childhood excursions that even there, in the heavy fighting, it was hard to believe what the Nazis had done. It made him furious. *This was what they did,* Jiri writes, now bending to the page again, addressing Markéta and Tika and Anna and also Marjorie Legnini—*what Hitler did, what the Communists did after him. They were determined to destroy any memory we had, you see? To put their vicious stamp on everything they touched. This is what such people do: They wipe out your memory, they replace it with their own. They want you to believe that your own history never existed, to loosen your moorings so that they can control you. So you must work to <u>remember</u>, even if they take your whole town away and make it nothing but wind and grass! Remember what life was like before their terror! Our country rebuilt the clock as it was, rebuilt Prague as it was, and I think of my home and I remember the Ferris wheel in front of the Lidice church when the fair came in fall and all of the people gathered there and the band music at night and a girl I flirted with at the wall when I was twelve. The Nazis destroyed all of it, but I remember it.*

The moth works at the window. The clocks chime softly together. One o'clock. Jiri looks down at the garage, the dark roof there. He thinks a moment and writes, *P.S. Anna, one of the hardest things for me is that I cannot drive anymore. It is one of the ways I am no longer of any help to you. I am hoping I'll be able to drive again. You have never thought of yourself as a good driver I know but you are actually a very good one and your only problem is that when you make left turns you jerk it, angle by angle, instead of making a smooth turn. This is a problem of concentration, not of driving, and I would not mention it except I am scared of it and we start getting cross with each other and shouting at each other in the car and I wish I handled it better. I just want you to concentrate and be safe, drahoušku. But I hope I will drive again.*

———

And now Jiri falls again into his history.

It is a few days before Christmas 1948. The sound of drenching rain through the glass. Jiri stands in the window of the SS Archival Room in the Palace of Justice, Nuremberg, watching the storm over the city. He is taking a break, allowing himself a well-deserved daydream. He has met a woman at the Válka camp for refugees; she flirts with him with her large blue eyes. Her name is Anna Šroubková and she has come in, a month before, from Slovakia, with her mother and cousin (the rest of her family was lost in the war, her father in the Prague uprising in 1945, in those same streets where Jiri fought). Jiri has told Anna once, full of emotion, that his family was from Lidice and that he has not found news of his mother and sister. And they have spoken no more of the dark times, as if agreed in the touch of hands that the tragedy is there but they must also live, move forward; she has made Jiri feel alive again. Sometimes he takes the tram across broken Nuremberg just to walk with her on the road from Válka to Soldier's Field. In that huge stadium, where Hitler once exhorted his robot troops to fight as one, where now threadbare couples stroll through with picnic baskets on warmer December days for lunch, Anna will laugh about the large blue ski coat she was issued, with its big arms that flop. Jiri has bought for her, for Christmas, a fine warm coat, and coats for her mother and cousin, too, and he cannot wait to give them these presents on Christmas Eve.

The city is dark beneath the suddenly fierce winter rain, and water flows freely in the areas cleared of rubble. People seem to walk endlessly through the thoroughfares, the rain darkening their shoulders. Jiri sees a man, both of his legs amputated, riding on the shoulders of a friend. Women in shawls walk briskly beneath the window; he sees buildings where windows are burned-out holes, chimneys standing with no structure around them, like fingers pointing at the sky. There is a gathering of prostitutes at a corner two streets away, huddled beneath the eave of a blackened building, waiting for evening customers.

It is as if the war never ended, as if the bodies of Adolf Hitler and Eva Braun still flicker with gasoline flames in the Chancellery garden. This is the Europe Hitler has left behind: these empty, crumbling shapes that beneath rain look like ancient ruins. Nine million human beings roam, finding what shelter they can. German teenage girls are raped by gangs of Polish orphans in alleys near the railroad stations. Jews are in a massive exodus (just this morning Jiri has walked by graffiti on this street reading, *Jude, verrecke! Croak, Jew!*), to France and the port of Haifa, and finally to their new country, which has been etched into history with violence. The darkness of Communism is strangling Czechoslovakia, sending those strong enough and brave enough, like Anna and those left of her family, over the Šumava Mountains to West Germany. Sometimes the Czech guides hired for these journeys are criminals who shoot their clients, leave them for dead, take suitcases with life savings. Jiri sets his jaw. He would like to meet such traitorous sons of bitches.

Dr. Kobera's group has come as an entire cell to Germany to assist United States intelligence, and the U.S. Army has requested Jiri's services on a steady basis, and he has, quite surprisingly, found that he has a career as a translator. He arrives, in civilian clothes, each day at the offices above and is then dispatched to Válka or to other nondescript buildings in Nuremberg; he interviews ordinary Czechoslovak citizens, and statesmen, and professors, helping counterintelligence create a constantly changing mosaic of the Czech nation with information from these refugees. *In what shape are the roads in your town?* he asks. *Are the bridges still functioning? Where have the Communists built military bunkers, do you know? How much do you know about the Communist dignitaries in your area? Can you tell us anything about any other military activities you have seen?* The refugees are paid eight marks for their information, and some wave off the money, saying it is only their patriotic duty to tell Jiri what they can; the hair-raising journey beneath the machine-gun towers and searchlights has left them furious that their home has, once again, been occupied.

Jiri shrugs his shoulders to release tension, turns his head from the winter window.

He has files here, spread across one of the long wooden tables, photographs taken by the precise SS to document their extermination of the inferior races of the world. He has gone through the photographs methodically from June 1942 on, a project so far of ten months, hoping against hope for a miracle, that he shall see his mother and sister somewhere, have, finally, an answer to how they perished. For he believes they are gone now, that somehow, with all of his searching, he would have found them. He is searching for himself, and for his father, to have answers.

Below him, a crime unfolds near the Baltic Sea: An SS trooper aims his rifle at a woman huddling with her child while frantic peasants dig a grave a few feet away. The huddling is efficient for the SS man; the woman and child can be killed with one shot. Jiri leans forward with the glass, looking carefully at the anguished faces of the peasants behind; there are some women, but none remotely resembling Jana or Helena. Soon enough, the mother and child are dead—a moment of the mother's body recoiling, the child falling, arms outstretched—the bodies quickly pulled and shoved into the grave, buried by the others. Then the peasants are shot as well. In another series Einsatzgruppen men sit and stand casually with rifles and pistols at the edges of death pits, where beneath them naked arms and legs are splayed, akimbo, in moments after shootings, some victims still alive. In a Russian city, an Einsatzgruppen killer beats a Russian woman savagely with a stick; the photograph catches the German with a grimace on his face as he delivers the death blows. Jiri goes over the faces of other prisoners watching nearby. Three women—none his mother or sister. A boy looks up in horror at his father, who strokes his head as the beating goes on. As hardened as he is, Jiri still catches himself full of emotion, and sometimes he can suddenly swear, especially seeing the children, their last moments on the earth visited by such horrors.

Here in a new set of prints women near the Baltic Sea lie naked on a knoll, a gentle sea of flesh. One of the Einsatzgruppen men who soon will kill them stands in the foreground, a dark figure with a rifle, a violent intrusion on the curving forms. Then he and other dark figures are firing, and there is blood from the women, some trying to run, and at the crest of the hill one woman has her arm protectively over another. Jiri looks carefully, but none of the faces in the foreground that he can make out belong to him; the women at the top of the hill are silhouettes against a white sky. Furious wind gusts at the window, a sudden drumming. Jiri looks up, and the glass is shuddering. He stands and walks to the window, and below in the street a prostitute is taking the arm of a man, and they huddle beneath an umbrella. The spokes of the umbrella are bending with the force of the wind.

Jiri goes on to the next file, marked *Ukraine*. After spending another futile hour with his magnifying glass, keeping careful note of those files he has looked through (a notebook now almost completely filled with identifying numbers and descriptions in his heavy pen), he takes his raincoat and shuts off the lights.

He has only a short journey home on the Autobahn, just outside the city, but he watches his speed; it feels idiotic, with other Germans speeding by him, but the MPs have lately been enforcing the 55 mph speed limit on cars with U.S. government plates to save fuel. He tries to push the dreadful SS images away from him—to leave them in that room, and to think only of the cardboard boxes he must ask his landlady for, for a neat job of packing the three Christmas coats—to think of Anna's eyes lighting at his attention to her family. He shall listen to his radio this evening, Sinatra and Benny Goodman; he shall wrap his presents. He plays the music every night; he needs the trumpet voice of Sinatra, the silk notes of Benny's clarinet to keep the horrific SS images at bay, just enough to sleep. Perhaps he will need, as he does sometimes, to drug himself with aspirin. The rain is letting up, and the night fog makes the trees here at the sides of the highway look like ghostly etchings. A moon is emerging from behind the clouds.

The moth insists at the screen. Jiri is on the St. Martin's roof over Lidice. He is working with Emile Hodja. In the street below Helena is riding her bicycle. It is fall. You cannot see her flesh, for she wears gloves and she is dressed in black, with a wide hat that hides her face, but Jiri is certain it is his sister, for he sees the bracelet on her wrist— the only color on her body. He is calling to her but she does not see him. She just keeps gliding over cobblestones, soundlessly, through a very empty Lidice. Behind him, Emile Hodja is whispering, fiercely, Jiri.

"*Jiri.*"

Jiri wakes. It does not make sense that the light is on at night, for the Nazis will see it, and there will be a harsh knocking at the door, terrible reprisals. Amazingly bright light. Everything is too immediate. The vinyl tablecloth—roosters set in a beige cross-hatched pattern—why in the hell hadn't he and Anna, in all of their years of marriage, gotten something a little more artistic to put on their table?

"*Jiri!*" Anna gently lifts his head from where it lies, on the book, the smell of the paper still in Jiri's nostrils, the pen still in his hand. The moth is trying for the light, bumping the screen. The light is too goddamn bright. He is not sure where his magnifying glass has gone to. It was here in his hand a moment ago.

"I've been looking," he says.

Anna sits next to him in her robe, staring at him through her glasses. She rubs his cheekbone, holds his jaw.

"I've been looking," Jiri repeats. Just a moment ago he saw those ghostly trees reaching through the fog.

"Are you all right?" Anna says. "Should we go to the hospital?"

Jiri thinks of nurses probing for his veins, the sharp pin of the needle going in. He hates the goddamn needles. Sitting in bloody waiting rooms, going into dimly lit bathrooms that smell of urine and antiseptic and men's sweat. The forced cheer of nurses, the occasional sharp arrogance of one doctor or another. He seems all right, for Christ's sake. He says so.

"Who is the president of the United States?" Anna says.

"I wish I didn't know," Jiri says.

"Jiri, *who?*"

"Daddy's boy. George W."

"What state are you in?"

"Massachusetts. We saw the fire performers this afternoon."

"Well, that's something, anyway," Anna says. "You gave me a scare." She strokes his cheek. "I'll put on some soup," she says.

And this is good now, better. He pushes his writing aside. What the hell was he thinking, writing like a madman? It happens sometimes now, that when he starts to feel he is recovering some function of brain or body, he immediately overdoes it. He needs to take it easy, breathe the cool evening, listen to the sound of his wife's voice.

Anna moves in her kitchen, speaking to him, as Jiri tries to collect his thoughts. It is September 2001, he tells himself. Many things are long past. Markéta is all right; she is in Seattle, and there is always a chance that she might come home with her job and husband—if he can find work here—in a year or so. Tika is on a date with Jesse, and he's a good kid, he's serious enough, he'll look after her. It seems Tika was here for dinner tonight but Jiri is a little uncertain of this. On the radio recently—tonight?—the NPR people were talking about that Washington intern who has disappeared. He feels for the poor damn parents. Hell, if it were Markéta or Tika, he would be on a crusade of no mercy. He would shake that congressman's neck until the guy spilled it. The son of a bitch.

They sit at the table with the lentil soup. Jiri tries to concentrate on the light conversation of his wife, tries not to think of the world of the dead, this place he hovers in now sometimes. He looks down to where his car is, is just beginning to form the words *I hope I'll be driving again soon* to Anna, when Anna suddenly is saying, "Wait, Jiri, I hear something. I just heard something." Her hand touches his forearm to silence him, and Jiri waits and then, through the night, they hear a woman scream.

THIRTEEN

Alison Tiner has left her door open, and Ghost-Man puts his groceries down on the outdoor step and takes out his legal package with the knife and unties the twine and goes right in after her.

The dark wood hallway smells of Alison: aloe and oils and glues, and of long days spent thinking about the position of things on canvas. There are tongue-and-groove thin-stained boards on the ceiling and walls here. A sharp smell of flowers, in a vase on the hall table. The meth seems to make his thighs sing, his shoulders float. He hears her in the kitchen, follows. She is turning on an overhead light, the grocery bag crackling as she sets it down on the counter. The kitchen is wide, with a butcher-block table, and Alison Tiner has turned—realizing that someone is directly following her. She drops the white bag she is holding and she is screaming, the rice splitting on the wood floor, hissing white and thin, and Ghost-Man is looking at it with horror, then holding up one hand as if in surrender, trying to explain.

"Just *listen*," he says as calmly as he can, in the midst of that female bellowing, that face contorting, lips drawn back away from teeth.

She screams, *"Get out get* out *of my house, oh my God get out—"*

The sound of Alison Tiner seems to explode through the room. He couldn't tell her about Christ before, about what it must have been like *to have had a Roman soldier with his knee holding down your elbow, driving a spike through your wrist.* To tell her about how if you took your lover to Brazil you would see the blood on the statues and maybe that would be good for you, to see reality instead of your little fucked-up yuppie Cambridge. It is hard to express everything, now that he's actually speaking to her; he finds that his voice is shaking. He is staring from her to that rice.

She is drawn back against the counter, yelling, *"Fire! Oh God, fire—"*

"Just *li*sten to me," Ghost-Man says, beginning to shout also. "I'll tell you just *one fuck*ing thing and then I'll *fuck*ing go, all right? *Fuck.* Just fucking listen."

But she is bunched against the corner where the microwave is, looking at him and screaming the torrent of words, and Ghost-Man tucks his package close to his side and purses his lips, feeling the muscles of his face quiver, and he walks by her and out the kitchen door to the backyard, down steps, behind the two garages and through a thicket of heavy-smelling sumac and into the shadows of buildings on Irving Street. He hears his breathing, looks down at his steady trousers, shoes, at bubblegum wrappers, a newspaper, a used condom, some tinfoil caught in the rusting old fence here where the chain link is bent back, the dark path going straight through. She is still screaming. *Crazy bitch.* In a minute he hears the blipping sirens of police cars coming onto Trowbridge; they glance through the trees. He walks onto the Irving sidewalk. Light blinks on in a brownstone above, and some people are coming out of the building to see what all the commotion is. He looks, too; through the foliage the buildings of Trowbridge Street are a march of windows, squatting beneath trees and telephone lines, lights coming on; he feigns curiosity. He looks just long enough to make it believable, shakes his head with some of those who have gathered—*What craziness is in the world now?*—then goes steadily toward the brightness of Kirkland Street, holding his package tightly.

The goddamn groceries are on the front step. Because I completely lost myself and didn't think. The goddamn soy milk bottle, the plastic on the Poland Spring six-pack with my fingerprints all over them. The police might overlook it at first, thinking she left it there; a helpful neighbor will bring it in for her, while the police are interviewing her, unload the soy milk and Poland Spring, the chili and apples, smudge up the prints maybe a little. And Alison will say, Those aren't mine, *and the neighbor will say,* But, dear, they were on the doorstep, *and Alison will look alarmed and say,* That's right, when he was beside me at the travel agency he had a grocery bag. *Soon they will know I am alive. They will then know about the other neighborhoods and the other women. Oh, fuck. Fuck fuck fuck.*

In his mind Ghost-Man can still hear Alison Tiner shouting, a sound that was unreal, deafening. The terrified white of her face. There is sweat at the sides of his throat, the small of his back. What had happened to his quickness and courage? Why hadn't he been prepared? It wasn't supposed to be like this! It was such a simple thing! *Fuck!* He just wanted to talk to her. To straighten a few things out!

He has recovered himself somewhat by the time he reaches the car. It is a year-old Mazda sedan, and it waits here beneath a spread of oaks on Summer Street next to a meter. The left front fender is dented and this embarrasses him—it happened in the city a few days ago, when he was parked, and of course nobody left a note. He should have gotten it fixed right away but he was lazy about it and now it is something that someone could identify him with. Things are falling apart, small things that will add up to very big problems. He needs to think. He ducks quickly into the car, puts his head back on the headrest, sits there in the darkness.

He might drive back to his small apartment in the bloodred brick building on George Street, in Medford, where he can turn on his computer, clutch himself through his pants, watching a film he has downloaded to his RealPlayer—this would be the smart thing to do. The film is short, all of two minutes: A man is naked, on his knees, his body bent forward. He is in an odd, dark room of shimmering curtains, a single door beyond him. A woman comes through the door wearing a long black leather dress, a black cape. It is hard to make out her movement, that strange, quirky streaming video that reminds Ghost-Man of images from the moon all those years ago: bodies moving through another gravity. The woman comes forward, and it is terribly, exquisitely quiet, and you hear the rustle of her dress, the click of her heels, feel her bristling *presence* in that room. She kicks the man, just once, hard, and pushes him with her shoe onto his side. She says, *You'll keep waiting*. She raises the cape with one arm and turns, walks from the room. The door closes.

Ghost-Man is clutching himself. He can go and relieve this, be in this protected, exalted simplicity, get away from the world. He can lie in his bed after and listen to college girls walk beneath his window, the lightness of their voices. A police car turns onto the street before him, lights wash through the glass, and he ducks away as if to check something on the seat. He takes his hand from his pants, starts the car, puts it into gear, and the police car whooshes by.

This is how it will be now. In his rearview mirror, the police car is at the intersection, brake lights flickering, turning harmlessly onto Cambridge. Ghost-Man drives in the opposite direction, starts moving down Kirkland Avenue. Past Gary's bar, then the spaghetti place with the neon display of fettuccine in the window, to the rise into Union Square, most of these stores darkened. A commuter train sparks over the bridge and then is gone into the night. The clock above the Somerville bank has its hands set at one forty-five. He swings left beneath the bridge, checks in the rearview mirror. No police. *But this is how it will be now.*

Fuck, fuck, fuck.

Once, in a desert battle, Simon held the head of his friend Harvey Stocker in his lap. But half of the head wasn't there. There was an eye, and then there was wet, bloody darkness. The other guys were saying, C'mon, Simon, he's fucking gone, let them take him. *There was a smell of cordite everywhere. The desert was like a weird ocean, tinted red, the sky red. Simon's M-16A2 was beside him and he wanted to pick it up and jam it into the gut of every Iraqi he could find and fire and fire.* Simon, Simon, Simon. Hey, Simon. Jesus Christ, Simon, let him go. *In the distance, Saddam's burning came from the throat of the earth, black-twisting clouds rising into the red.*

Ghost-Man rolls up onto the highway, thinking of Harvey Stocker, Harvey tough and firing into that red horizon, saying, *Simon, man, holy shit oh fuck*—in that moment before the bright white light, the crack of explosion, the screaming everywhere.

FOURTEEN

Fuck. These potholes, all over the goddamn place. Ghost-Man hurtles down Route 38, thinking, *With all the goddamn taxes everyone is paying someone should work on these.* He is angry that the fucking rice spooked him, now as all of it is coming back, that he lost his nerve. He has a lot to tell the woman, and he shouldn't have let her hysterics affect him that way.

Now over the bridge, wheels sounding like thunder on the grating, by malls, lights out, swinging left with the highway, running parallel to Route 93. It would be easy to go north, to 95 and to Maine. He remembers Jenna kayaking with him near Kittery, her eyes delighted as the sea rose with her, and at the shore behind her white fans of spray.

Ghost-Man turns in at the Burger King, across from the Century Bank, pulls the Mazda swiftly into the S-curve drive-through, waiting behind a rusting white van to order. There is a mother with her children in the van; Ghost-Man sees silhouettes through windows against the bright orange neon. It takes a while for them to order, the mother turning back to admonish and request and plead and snap, then turning to the monitor again, and Ghost-Man hears, "Three number twos, um, can I have a Diet Coke and two milks and two Crispy Chicken Meals and one Whopper Junior." He looks up at the Burger King sign above, a circular medallion of red and orange—an American fire cartoon set against the autumn night. Ghost-Man is remembering. *In a helicopter above the desert there are just the other guys with him now and no Harvey Stocker, hard to believe no fucking Harvey, and far below them charred corpses and war machines and buses and cars are scattered on the highway, mile after mile, and someone says,* Holy shit, you guys, it's like the end of the fucking world, *and on the horizon Saddam's oil fires are burning and burning. Father Bush is pulling America out of the war, leaving those who have defied the dictator, Shiite and Kurds, to be butchered. The flames lick the sky with impunity, like they will burn forever.*

Ghost-Man eases the car forward to order. In the windows of the restaurant are slate blue plastic tubes that children can crawl through while parents are wolfing down late night dinners. What's the world coming to when children stay up so late and parents don't even think twice about it? Ghost-Man orders a Diet Coke and a BK Broiler without mayonnaise, for lately he has been trying to lose weight. You hit forty, the jowls start to sag with the belly, and it's murder to try to keep it off, even with all the walking he does. He motors up to window two and pays four dollars and eighteen cents, the sunshade dropped over his face, hoping that the cheery Hispanic woman there does not see much of him or his dented car as it slides past her window.

He eats in the parking lot of the Admiral a few blocks down, close to 93. It is an old converted bikers' bar, and men's cars are packed here, parked in close to the building, the neon sign an artist's curvy girl with an admiral's cap, saluting, her oversize elec-

tric lips glistening red, bright cursive reading *Live Dancing Late*.
High above Ghost-Man, to this side of the building, is the huge
billboard, set so that you can see it from 93, of Kascha LaFond's
enormous eyes advertising expensive gin. There is a silver-colored
bottle, and letters, five feet tall, across the bottom: *BOMBAY SAP-
PHIRE GIN: BECAUSE SHE IS WATCHING.* The eyes probe for
male prowess. Ghost-Man glances at the constant rush of cars on
the highway, thinks of the men in those cars seeing Kascha, these
eyes so famous that they alone are recognizable, this glance of a
wary gatekeeper. Men thinking of scenarios that might let them
impress such a woman, quickly, for it is not hard to imagine her
slipping from probing and flirting to an untouchable indifference.

That is where the horror begins, Ghost-Man knows, in that moment when you think you will never be allowed to move in that
other flesh, in any female flesh, you might be counted out, no egg
for the sperm. *You make other fires.* He watches the traffic lights at
the turn to the highway burn in the September night, red and then
green: the Admiral's girl burns. He watches the provocative eyes
above, held up by rusty scaffolding.

Simon Jacob Acre went to work for, then eventually took over, Harvey Stocker's family business in Portland, Maine—made it, with
the family's blessing, into a small local empire. He kept the name,
always, *Harvey's Cleaning Services,* even when the business had ex-
panded to include all of the government buildings and most of the
major businesses downtown, and more extensive services—power
washing of exteriors and cleaning up after fires. In four years' time
he went from having eight employees to seventy-three.

He met his Jenna with her extraordinary green eyes there and built a home by the sea. She left her temp job at the Portland Bank soon after the marriage. Their home was made of Pennsylvania barn wood, with a great stone fireplace that everyone gathered around during their many parties. From the living room you could walk onto the cool veranda, torches illuminating circles of dark flagstone, women in their dresses holding fluted glasses of wine. Beyond the lawn and outcroppings of rock there was the sea, a dark whispering mirror of God.

In Ghost-Man's mind now he sees his Jenna, a month before she came to him and asked him for the divorce. It is a night of festivity—a birthday party for a dear friend of hers who is a local politician, a woman whom Simon is actively engaged in a conversation with when he looks across the room at his wife. Jenna is in a gray chiffon dress and satin sandals, and Simon is thinking of how elegant his wife is when she puts down her wineglass. The man she is talking to is making her laugh; she covers her face with her hands, and her eyes flirt. She laughs again with her long throat, her blond hair tossed back, touches the man's wrist with her fingers.

It burns like a hot wire in him, that evening. The politician, taking him by the arm, led him out to the veranda, and her empathy told Ghost-Man how long ago he had lost his wife. *If I ever had her,* he thought. *If it wasn't only about money. The things, the security I could bring into her life.* He watched the sea beneath the moon; he imagined his wife's face in a hotel bed, beyond another male shoulder, her eyes closed in ecstasy.

He keeps the windows of the Mazda down, finishing his chicken sandwich. Thinks of turning on the radio and then decides against it. He must assume it will be only hours before they know who they are after. There will be older photographs from the military, of course, and some of him in *Portland Business Magazine* and newspaper files. So tonight he must pack a few things, inconspicuously (he is always ready for flight), and then with one of the other license plates and identities he has prepared he must drive west. He has wanted to see Nevada; he can be there for a brief, quiet time and then fly to Europe or perhaps the Caribbean. He is feeling better. *Just no more stupid fucking mistakes.* Ghost-Man checks his teeth in the mirror closely, a horseshoe of white, fillings, glistening saliva—finds a breath mint in the glove compartment. He stuffs the Burger King bag with its wrappings under a seat, tightly, reminding himself to pull it out later and vacuum the car. He leaves his package on the seat beside him, beneath a windbreaker (they will not let him in with the package), locks the car, and walks to the cement-block building, this paint fading and peeling as you get up close to it. The heavy rock music from the club catches Ghost-Man's heart, and the air is cool on his arms; just above him the Admiral girl salutes with her neon brightness.

FIFTEEN

The iron-barred doors are wide open, and beyond them is another set of glass doors and a bouncer with a blue T-shirt saying *Security* who greets Ghost-Man with a thin smile, and a woman beside the bouncer, bleached blond, fortyish, who sits behind a small desk. She puts a cigarette in her mouth and takes Ghost-Man's ten dollars and gives him a ticket and five in change and says, "Thanks," without meaning it. She takes a drag of her cigarette and blows it out and looks out at the parking lot and Route 38, the whizzing of cars there. Ghost-Man puts his change in his wallet, and the woman waits for him to be gone so that she can resume her discussion with the bouncer. Ghost-Man slides his ticket into the wallet, too, imagining the peroxide blonde at the mirror in the morning, angry at the wrinkles, at gravity robbing her of whatever power she once had—a once pretty, now hard face, pinched in bitterness. Perhaps she was a dancer once, also; it is always the story with certain women who make consistent, dumb decisions about men. They tell their friends this is *it*, they are in love: He is handsome, he drives a beautiful car, he has a solid blue-collar job.

Perhaps they get pregnant on purpose when the guy isn't coming around as fast as they want him to, and then are surprised at the first fist blows. Surprised that this man who took their breath from them, who seemed to care for them and almost *willed* them into love, can now be so indifferent to them and to his own children. And all the while there are good men, nearby, waiting; but these kinds of women always want something else, some talk-show version of life. They are doomed, these females, perhaps by their history, certainly by the decisions they make. But still they fill you with hope, when they are young, when their bodies move so gracefully. They make you want to bring them things, to lay gifts of possibility at their feet.

Past the glass doors, after the brightness of the highway and then the entrance, the club is in a darkness from which female forms emerge. Ghost-Man sees a curvaceous naked leg, here to the left, rising above the dark silhouettes of staring men, and there to the right, an undulating female back beneath whirling tracer lights of blue and red. Ghost-Man's timing is good; on the center stage, beneath a high, glinting disco ball, Velvet Queen is moving in a black sheer gown, a dark veil over her face. Ghost-Man takes a seat at the left stage, a circle surrounded by a brass rail, for Velvet Queen will be here next, when her set on the main central stage is done. He orders from the waifish, knock-kneed waitress a rum and Coke, and turns on his stool and watches a dancer a few feet from him, in a circle of twenty-some other men, a delightfully pale woman called Autumn, red-haired, with dark red lips. The waitress comes with his drink, smiling at him, because he always tips well: Ghost-Man gives her his customary six dollars. From here he can look over the whole bar, and as his eyes adjust he sees that there are men everywhere, surrounding the stages so deeply that, across the room, where a dancer is lying on the floorboards of the far right stage, he can see only her legs, a long, tapered show rising above the patrons. The place is a dark circus, a constantly moving vision of shadows and color and haunted faces, the many voices a drone beneath Hootie & the Blowfish singing "Let Her Cry."

Ghost-Man watches Velvet Queen as she sits back on the center stage, leaning on hands, her gown and veil off now. She wears only tall black vinyl boots, and she spreads her legs very slowly for three college guys who have put a group of dollars on the brass rail. She crooks her finger at them and they lean forward eagerly, their faces transformed; it is as if she has brought them all back to Little League, and they've hit a ball solidly with the sweet spot of a bat, and they are watching that moment of effort and intuition soar into the sky. They laugh at what she tells them, and her mock sensuality is momentarily broken, she's acting *friendly,* they're thinking, *She's great, why the fuck can't we* meet *women like this?* And in that moment she sweeps forward, takes their dollars, and rises and throws their money to the end of the stage.

And now, a few minutes later, she has come to this stage, the small platform before Ghost-Man, dressed again in the sheer gown, dark underwear beneath but no veil, and as she steps up she lays a hand on Ghost-Man's shoulder and whispers into his ear, "Hi, Simon. Hi, baby." He murmurs his hello, and something about whether she is having a good night, and she nods and grazes his ear with her fingers and steps onto the circular, polished wood with her dancer's grace; she takes command, so tall in the boots, the light coming through the gown from above, outlining her wonderful form. She starts moving to Linda Ronstadt, *"Feeling better, now that we're through / Feeling better 'cause I'm over you . . ."* and the song gives Ghost-Man an image from his first year in the army; on

leave in Georgia, a college girl taking him back to her dorm, moving above him in bed quietly and with intensity, the roommate
asleep on the other bunk. He remembers the heavy smell of alcohol in the room, the taste of Aquafresh toothpaste in the girl's
mouth. Some sort of river winding through the campus, a dark S
outside the window.

There is a man close to Ghost-Man who has gained the weight
of the American male in his thirties, and on his left hand is a wedding ring. He has put a five-dollar bill on the rail, and he looks up
expectantly and Ghost-Man, watching him, sipping the rum and
Coke, believes he can feel the rise in the chest, the catch in the
throat, that the married man does, with Velvet Queen now focused
on him. *She knows. Knows the dark center of us. A man cannot hide
when she watches you.* She looks down at the married man, the long
breadth of her so stunning that for a moment Ghost-Man feels as
if he is suspended, somehow, in space; she tilts her head a little at
the man, as if to say, *What can we do for* you? Velvet Queen lies
down before him with her legs very wide, pulls the gown away from
her body, and some of the men surrounding Ghost-Man groan. She
has one hand supporting her head, and her eyes do not leave those
of the married man. She moves her other hand between her legs,
runs a long finger over the fabric of her underwear; her fingers
deftly move her underwear to the side, and she lightly touches that
pink fold of flesh. She lets the panties snap back into place and
pulls down the sheer bra and brings a breast up to her mouth,
touching a tongue to nipple, watching the married man all the
time, and then she smiles to break the spell she has created, and
takes the five, turns, and, watching the man over her shoulder,
tosses the bill toward the short flight of stairs. The man settles
back into his seat, swigging his beer, staring up as Velvet Queen

turns to another patron. There is the opening of the man's spirit, the moment of hope the man lives in now that will collide with reality somewhere on the ride home. But the small fire that Velvet Queen has set in him will take a day, maybe two, to die out, and then the man will be back to replenish it.

Ghost-Man drinks. The rum and Coke makes him feel a little better about Alison Tiner, her manic yelling in that close kitchen. He let the fucking rice spook him, that was it, but his reaction—to just walk out the back fucking door once he had taken the plunge, to expose himself to danger—was unacceptable. So the girls here, Velvet Queen, must fortify him, ease him, *she* and *she* and *she* and *she*. He pulls the five-dollar bill from his wallet and lays it on the rail as Velvet Queen dances on the opposite side of the circle; in his wallet are a fifty-dollar bill, and a ten and a few ones, and he will need to break up the fifty for more change, for a twenty, so that after one more meth Velvet Queen can take him by the hand into the VIP room and dance over him, straddle him on the couch, brush his chest with her breasts, and whisper words to him as he smiles with embarrassment or retreats within himself, his eyes with her but also far away, and *anything is all right with her, even (especially) when she holds his arms tightly at the shoulders or wrists, pinning him to the couch, and he whimpers and groans.* Now she turns to him with these extraordinary violet eyes, now she lies naked but for the panties, and she dips a leg over the railing, a vinyl boot, and lets it graze Ghost-Man's shoulder. This earns him respectful glances from the other men, for Velvet Queen has not touched *them* (*"I'm gonna say it again / You're no good / You're no good / You're no good / Baby, you're no good . . ."*), and Velvet Queen has her legs on either side of Ghost-Man, her body undulating, teasing, and his face, his mouth and eyes, his limbs, seem foolish.

The lights move over her and Ghost-Man can hardly swallow. Oh
if. *If* she could do this each day for him, each evening, he could be
harmless. Could tend to this fire and no others. He could live in
this shock of black hair, these playful, cruel eyes that consider
what the grazing of her leg against his shoulder, his cheek, can do;
she watches his chest, his eyes, as if they are parts of some great
experiment she is conducting. Ghost-Man's throat is dry. He
knows what a fool he looks like—a man approaching the heart of
middle age, not yet thick or thin, nothing a woman this age would
ever be interested in. Yet he cannot help letting himself go; in these
moments with her, he hardly knows who he is. She wets her lips of
bloodred. Is it his imagination, or does she always spend a little
more time with him than the other customers? She spreads her
legs for him, her back arched, the nipples pointing up, her black
hair brushing floorboards. This vulva encased in sheer black, teasing. Then she flips up on her knees and comes close to his face as
she takes the bill, watching his eyes, saying, "*Thank* you, baby. See
you a little later, Simon?" and he recovers enough dignity to say, "A
little later," and leans back again.

Velvet Queen lies back on the floorboards. Behind her, directly
across from Ghost-Man, two men have arrived, pushing into the
crowd. One is slightly heavy, the other more solidly built, more
drunk, with a mustache. She leans back in the circle and holds out
her hands to the men, waggling her fingers playfully for money, and
the drunk one, the one with the mustache, holds a ten-dollar bill
above her, baiting her, and then leans down and whispers something into her ear.

Ghost-Man looks down at Velvet Queen's stomach muscles, the
light playing over her belly, and realizes suddenly that those muscles are not moving erotically, but functionally, rippling with the

effort: She is raising herself. Her face is furious and she is beginning to weep, and some men behind Ghost-Man are saying, *"What
the fuck?"* And the drunk man's grin has gone from knowing to a
feigned confusion, the boy after high school caught smoking a
joint, *What did I do?* And then three bouncers are on him and he is
saying, "Just a money-grabbing bitch, what the fuck did I do?" And
Velvet Queen is screaming, *"Motherfucker!"* standing now, pointing
at the man, her ass and thighs above Ghost-Man shaking, then
holding her arms to her body as if cold, in tears, and Ghost-Man is
standing, looking at Velvet Queen being led offstage by a bouncer
and another dancer, and the other bouncers are pushing the drunk
out the door, "Okay, okay, what the fuck? I didn't even fucking
touch her!" And Ghost-Man looks at Velvet Queen who, going up
to the bar now, is being comforted by the other dancer, Autumn,
who hugs her and strokes her hair. More dancers are coming over,
and he catches Velvet Queen saying, "He said it so close to me,
right into my fucking ear, so fucking vulgar, I just couldn't fucking
listen to it—" Another dancer quickly takes Velvet Queen's place in
the ring, but Ghost-Man is not paying attention. There is a rushing
whisper in his head. He tightens his jaw and moves directly
through the glass doors into the parking lot.

Beneath Kascha's eyes, leaning in the darkness against the scaffolding, the drunk man and his heavier friend are lighting cigarettes, laughing, giving each other the high-five. The clapping of
the hands makes something in Ghost-Man's heart snap, and he is
walking for them. He sees the drunk turning, lighting the cigarette,
black eyes of amusement as they turn to him, the friend staring
hard, in a blue baseball cap, and Ghost-Man slaps the cigarette
from the drunk's lips and hits him with an elbow to the teeth, and
the drunk goes down, writhing, and the heavy friend has Ghost-

Man by the neck, and, in a fury, Ghost-Man takes one fleshy forearm and judo flips the man hard onto the tar; he turns and the
drunk is up and holding a switchblade, looking frightened but
coming forward, and Ghost-Man takes the thrusting arm and
breaks it at the wrist, then snaps it at the elbow, and the drunk is
screaming and Ghost-Man twists him until he is on the ground,
the knife beside his head. Ghost-Man picks it up, points it into the
man's ear.

"Whoa—" his friend says, rasping there, up on his knees. He
holds up his hands. "Just fucking take it easy, man. He's an idiot
fucking drunk. You win."

Ghost-Man hears the man beneath him breathing hard, groaning at his broken arm. He thinks of Velvet Queen, shaking, her
sorry arms holding her body tight, the streak of tear down the side
of her face when she fell onto the shoulder of the other stripper.
He pushes the knife, hard and quickly, through the head, and the
mouth of the drunk opens and screams, screaming jaw, and the
metal tip of the knife strikes the pavement.

Then Ghost-Man is driving down 38 again, under the streetlights,
blood smearing his steering wheel. The friend in the baseball cap
had retched when Ghost-Man passed the knife through the head,
retched and then run, still puking, and Ghost-Man pulled out the
knife and stood up from that bloody head and checked around to
see if anyone was looking—nobody was—and stepped over the
body and walked calmly to his car.

His mind is busy now, busy with the thought of Alison Tiner and
what he needs to say to her. It is amazing that he was so fucking
docile about it the first time, just walking out the door like that

while she screamed. It is not too late to talk with her, to provide some intelligence, some reason; her boyfriend's flight is in by now, and perhaps Ghost-Man has about two hours before she is fucked, the man using her need of closeness and protection as an excuse to penetrate her. And she will be anxious to wrap her boyfriend in pussy! What a further opportunity to tether him! He can wait for them in*side* the apartment; he can ascertain when the boyfriend goes into the bathroom, before the fucking. Ghost-Man will try to get hold of Alison Tiner then and talk some sense to her. He knows he will need to subdue her, to keep her quiet, and then he can have his say. He has a flannel shirt in the backseat—he can cut a sleeve off for a gag, twist it tight behind her head. He imagines the cloth in Alison Tiner's teeth, stopping her insane screaming, what he should have done before, how things would have been different. If the boyfriend comes out to fight Ghost-Man will have to deal with him. But that will go quickly. If Ghost-Man is too late, and they are already fucking, he will have to deal with that. Then he has three-quarters of a tank of gasoline in a can, in the trunk, and he can finish the situation.

He would like to wash his hands. It is terrible, this stickiness, reminding him every fucking moment. The bloody knife is on the rubber mat beneath him, and before leaving Somerville he stops at an empty shopping center and tosses it down a storm drain. He drives, wiping his hands on his pants, the spaghetti place and a darkened Gary's bar going by to his left. Moving over the Cambridge line now; he will wait in Alison Tiner's darkness with those paintings, with parts of Alison Tiner redone in a million different configurations: Alison Tiner's fractured face across the canvas, fractured hands on floating chest, throat. Alison masturbating. The painted man howling into the darkness, the three women about him. There is a taste in Ghost-Man's mouth like strange copper. He turns left, hand over sticky hand, onto Trowbridge.

And here in front of Alison's apartment are two police cars, dark and shining. Ghost-Man swallows his surprise. He drives carefully by the cruisers, averting his face; he goes left onto Cambridge Avenue, pulls a wide U-turn. He parks at the curb beside Trowbridge Academy and then, the Mazda idling, looks across the school lawn at the buildings of Trowbridge Street. He is imagining scenarios, considering, but it is hard to think now because his legs and hands tremble with a constant, unquenchable need for motion.

SIXTEEN

Tika and Jesse take the clean cement steps heading down into Club Isis; the walls are cool blue, lit by hanging Moroccan antique lamps. The floor is filled with dancers, mostly college students, many of them stunning, dark Arabian women, all moving to the music of the group Bastet—a techno-pounding with female voices sailing over the rhythm. There is a smell of musk perfume and sweat and alcohol, and the bar, there in relative brightness to the left, is of beautiful blond wood, sparkling under pinholed goatskin lamps.

Jesse, with Tika in tow, searches throughout the club for Kerig and his girl, pushing through bodies to tables, and then Kerig is waving them over and, shouting, introduces them to a girl beside him named Saqqara. She has beautiful dark eyes, a white dress; she smiles up, offering a cool hand. They cannot talk over the music. Kerig shrugs and says, "Too loud," and Jesse takes both of Tika's hands and leads her onto the dance floor, and she is laughing and protesting that she needs to put down her case, but she gives up and raises her arms, and beneath huge palm fronds that stretch over them she moves her body, watching Jesse's eyes, sometimes laughing at him because for a musician he has very little style on the dance floor.

American faces move by her, bodies graze up against her, but the most beautiful are those of the Arabian women. They wear silver rings and large hoop earrings. Their makeup is exquisitely done to bring out dark eyes; their teeth, in contrast with coffee skin, are a brilliant white. Many have the black cloth belts with silver coins that accentuate their hips, and Tika imitates the way their arms go up in the air, offering balance to their bodies. She has seen the Bastet videos in lounges at Emerson; the Egyptian girl group has a big college following, and a lot of women are wearing these belts with the silver coins now. Susan has said that there is a place on Newbury Street that sells them, and Tika tells herself that she will get one. She catches Jesse looking closely at one young woman, his mouth a little open, and slaps his chest with the back of her hand. He gives a mock protest, which she cannot hear above the music. She puts her arms up around his shoulders and draws his ear down and says, "Behave yourself, sailor, and you might just get some later," and he holds up his hands as blinders, to block out all the Arabian women, then looks with hope at Tika, and she laughs and nods her head approvingly.

When the song ends she takes Jesse's hand and they go back to the table. Tika motions that she will get drinks, and Jesse leans down to Saqqara and Kerig, but they point to the drinks they still have and wave him off, saying, "Thanks." The music is deafening again, and Tika puts her camera case on the seat next to Jesse. She goes alone to the bar. She knows that Jesse will have a Coors; she will have white wine. She leans over the shining wood to give her order, and the bartender, an Irish-looking redhead with a tired face and heavy crow's-feet, nods and turns to get the drinks, and Tika digs into her pants pocket for cash. There are suddenly men all around her, dark like the women and some with a growth of beard; they wear cotton and silk shirts, pressed slacks, leather boots. She feels them staring. One tries to speak with her, but she gestures helplessly at the music speakers; she takes the drinks back, moving through their bodies, through the staccato of their language. Their eyes watch her. The bottle and glass are cool in her fingers, and she concentrates on this until she is away from them. At the table she drinks and leans close to Jesse; smells his neck, his Jesse-ness, his Aqua Velva aftershave, like cedar. Saqqara has her thin fingers on Kerig's, stroking, and she smiles at Tika. It would be nice to be sitting at an outdoor café with this woman, watching her skin and hair in that light. This would be in the Back Bay; beside them a flower shop would have pots of white and indigo roses on the sidewalk, and Tika would hear Saqqara's voice above the sound of the sidewalk crowd, the cars going by. She would like this, learning about this woman—she must ask Kerig for her number.

Kerig is shouting something across the table about a recording machine, and Jesse is trying to make it out; close by, some Latino girls dance together, dark tube tops and fashionable jeans and heels. Then the Latino girls are separating, applauding, men applauding beside them as eight professional belly dancers come through the crowd. Above, on the wall, Isis spreads her wings; the belly dancers here form a circle. There is growing applause as the song fades and in its place comes a high-pitched instrumental, and the women draw arms from beneath sheer gowns and the audience claps now in rhythm with them, whistles. The dancers play finger cymbals; they move in practiced synchronicity to Egyptian bamboo flutes and tambourines. They dance barefoot, veiled. Tika and

Jesse and Saqqara and Kerig are up and standing close, clapping in rhythm with the audience. Tika loves the practiced positions of the women's hands and arms—the mystery of lips and eyelashes that brush at the veils. The tight, choreographed circles: hips and shoulders and hands. Each circle seems to worship an invisible center. She wants to dance like that. She wants to be home in bed with Jesse, her knee pushing between his legs, opening him up. Soon, when the dancers are done and she has danced a little more with Jesse, she will ask him to go, and together they will hurtle home in the subway darkness, her fingers inside his jacket; she will breathe the smell of his neck.

The dancers spin: quick, breathtaking profiles beneath the veils, gowns sweeping. Tika watches bracelets falling on brown forearms, finely shaped hands, and fingers snapping with cymbals in precise, golden circles of light.

SEVENTEEN

S*on of a bitch,* Jiri thinks, looking through the magnifying glass. In the SS photographs the Einsatzgruppen killer raises a heavy stick, his face one of righteous fury. He is beating a woman, perhaps in her forties, who kneels on the ground, and you can see that his anger comes from the fact that she keeps trying to get up. He is aiming toward her head; in her last moment of life she is bleeding from the mouth, weeping.

Son of a bitch.

The wind moans outside the palace; a gust hits the windows with a spray of rain. Jiri looks up, watches the glass flex slightly with the force of the storm: a bending of light. He stares again carefully through the magnifying glass at the last picture of the series—the woman now lies on the ground, the killer over her—and then shakes his head with sadness and stacks the photographs together (each stamped *Ukraine, 1942*) and slips them back into a manila file.

He picks up another file marked *East Prussia, Baltic Sea, June 17, 1942.* Here are women, perhaps one hundred strong, being marched to a knoll, a white sky beyond. The Einsatzgruppen seem to be everywhere, herding, pushing with submachine guns and rifles. Jiri imagines the fast, drunken voices of the soldiers shouting, *Eile! Move it!* The women are ordered to strip: Jiri, staring through his glass, can almost hear the female voices, like a flock of helpless birds—*So what, these drunken brutes will rape us now?*— and the angry German through a bullhorn, *Stille! Stille! We will burn your filthy clothes and give you new ones and then we will bring you to a containment camp!* Undressed, the women clutch arms about their bodies. Near the camera, one woman has blood matting the inside of her thighs and an Einsatzgruppen guard looks at her bloody flesh with disgust. Jiri pores over the women's faces with his glass: faces of terror, many profiles, a number of them turned away so that he cannot see their features. He does not see his sister or mother.

The women are ordered onto the knoll, facedown. Then, in the chronological run of images, the Nazis are dark figures, intruding, some with guns fixed on the women, some holding gasoline cans. And the women realize that they will be killed and they are starting to get up and run, but most are shot as they rise. Some make it a few steps. At the top of the hill, two women are frantic silhouettes; one has her arm protectively over the other, and then the one being protected is shot and falling. Staring through his glass, Jiri sees that the forearm of the falling woman seems slightly disjointed, a streak of black there moving away from the form of the arm. Is it a bullet passing through the arm, breaking the bone? A flaw in the negative? A diving gull on the horizon beyond?

Wind hits the palace window again, hard. The shuddering is so loud it seems the glass will tear from the framing. Jiri, startled, gets up and walks there, where clouds, lit by the city, rush at him. Rain pounds on the glass, but the window remains intact. On the street below, a prostitute and her client huddle and walk quickly beneath an umbrella.

Trowbridge Street, Cambridge, Massachusetts:
September 11, 2001, 1:50 A.M.

Anna and Jiri have dressed in jackets before coming out, and Jiri holds Anna close and taps with his cane as they walk. Now the harsh, revolving police lights outside Alison Tiner's doorway seem to completely alter reality: Jiri sees faces lit by white, falling into blackness, white again. Here are Monica Wood, and Heather Stolz, both with expressions of concern, staring at the door. There are some neighbors whose names he does not know. Alison's van is idling, with Ralph Topalka at the wheel, the curve of his neck and shoulder there, and Jiri hears Ralph speaking to a police officer. The white washes over the number on Alison's door, 37, and there are dark shapes and shadows of bushes and sunflowers, bright, then black. Jiri feels the closeness of the neighbors, the tightening of them as more arrive, the murmur of their voices, *Someone got in Alison's house, we heard her screaming. She was just coming back with groceries. She's all right, but really shook up. She's inside with Vivian.*

The door opens now, and Alison Tiner comes out, a cotton shawl held over her shoulders by Vivian Topalka. The image blinks, the two women black against a white background: Vivian holding Alison's shoulders. And in that moment, Jiri remembers the women on the knoll, struggling to run; he remembers his photograph of Jana and Helena in Lidice, his mother's arm over Helena. And he knows, with an intake of breath, why he wrote so much this night, went back in his memory to those SS photographs: that strange, small dash moving out from the forearm that had puzzled him—had it been a broken bone? A blemish on the negative, a seagull behind?

Or a bracelet.

The SS image comes back to him with startling clarity: the woman doing the protecting, the specific tilt of shoulders, of head. The slighter woman beneath her arm. These were Jana and Helena; he is suddenly sure of it. A fierce wind on the Nuremberg Palace windows had taken him from this truth, but now, watching Alison get into the back of a police cruiser with Vivian, now he remembers and knows.

He stands there, full of this light and horror. Imagining Jana grasp Helena's hand to run at the sounds of rifles being cocked, women's voices around them a burst of hysterics. Explosions of vicious sound and blood and flesh flaying about and Jana and Helena up and Jana throwing an arm around Helena and bullets biting into Helena's neck and head and torso and Jana screaming *Nay nay nay* and then wasps of fire at Jana's jaw, her forehead, her throat.

Jiri's hand grips Anna's tightly, and she says, "Jiri?"

He shakes his head. "No, later."

In the old black-and-white photographs, when he'd returned to them from the window that evening in Nuremberg, the female bodies, the curves of torn, human flesh, were doused with fuel, some of the women still alive, and set afire. The fire trembled against the horizon.

Jiri watches the police car, the van, another police car leave. Anna is urging him forward, for the crowd is dispersing. Jiri will not tell her right away. She sees that he is subdued but chalks it up, he believes, to what has just happened here, in the neighborhood. She is saying something, that this is all very dangerous. He wants the certainty of morning before he speaks of his mother and sister: the wall of daylight holding off darkness, night, before he makes it all completely real by telling his wife.

They go back to bed and after forty minutes his wife sleeps, and Jiri, his heart filled with grief, rises and puts on pants and a flannel shirt and the jacket and his shoes. He takes his cane and keys and locks the door and goes down the elevator to the back exit, to the garage, turns on lights, these bulbs shining above him; he stands in the dew-wet, cement-smelling space, his Buick clean there, a heavy red metal shadow. The bulbs throw black shapes all around him. He imagines daybreak, Anna listening to his memory of the SS images with her steady, believing eyes; she will go into the living room to call Shelley and tell her the situation, that she will not be in to work. Perhaps she will call Marjorie Legnini. Maybe Tika will come by during the day, too. That would be good, to see Tika. He opens the hood and checks the oil and the windshield fluid, then shuts the hood as quietly as possible and opens the driver's-side door and gets in, his hands tight on the steering wheel.

Wasn't Tika here earlier this evening? He *thinks* so. She had dinner with them. And why the devil were they just standing at Alison's doorway? God*damn*it, he cannot remember. He remembers the photographs, though, all those years ago on that winter night. Nuremberg. His mother and Helena against the sky. Burning.

The car feels musty—air closed here for too long—and he is crying like a goddamn baby. *Son of a bitch*. He could kill those Nazi bastards now as freshly as he did in the months, the three years, after Lidice. He puts his forehead on the steering wheel. His chest shakes with the ragged emotion, and he tries for a deep breath, but he cannot stop the shaking.

The garage looks like a kaleidoscope of light and dark: a shape of hedge clippers on the wall, a shovel, a rake. He leans back against the headrest, trying to gain some control of himself. He closes his eyes and sees Lidice: the village below him just before he entered the forest that last night.

He gets out of the Buick and walks out onto the driveway, back and forth, sometimes holding his head, the light of the garage casting his shadow in an arc against the chain-link fence at the end of the property. He can hear his mother's voice quite clearly, talking with his father in the garden: *Co se mu stalo? What has happened with Jiri?* He can see his mother's face, her eyes turning to him. He hears his sister mixing dumplings in the kitchen, the sounds of cicadas on the hill that goes down to the Horák farm. He goes around to the front of the apartment building and walks the sidewalk, speaking in Czech to himself, talking to his mother and father and sister. It is only after a long while that he is able to breathe a little more steadily.

EIGHTEEN

On the Coast of Maine: September 1996

Simon Jacob Acre turns on the lights of his house, kneels to the gasoline can, removes the cap. He gets up and pours a line on the blue-and-beige-patterned rug, over the armchairs facing each other, the duvet between them. There is a repeating call from a bird outside, the sound of the ocean below on the rocks, restless in early twilight. He pours past the cane dining table and onto a wall by the French doors. He opens the French doors to the sun porch, sweeps a bit of gas there. Up the stairs then, pouring as he goes, into the master bedroom, standing on the old bench at the foot of the bed, splashing the gasoline heavily onto the mattress, onto the walls, the floral-patterned draperies. He imagines the firemen saying to an open-eyed Jenna, *It started in the bedroom.* Oh, please God they tell her this. The gallon is empty; he throws it onto the bed. He steps through the sliding door onto the wide, screened-in sitting porch. The ocean is there, darkening, a crest of light at the horizon. He feels, suddenly, expansive; he has been living within the horror of Jenna's infidelity for five weeks now, and it can be over with this, with pulling the cloth from his pocket that he has weighted with a heavy, small piece of wood. He sets it aflame and imagines Jenna's eyes in disbelief—it cannot be that the man who always tried so hard to please her has this kind of fury in him. The news people will come interview the neighbors; Mrs. LaRoe, next door, will say, *He was such a quiet, hardworking man, I can't believe it.*

He throws the flame and there is a last near moment of silence, the unassuming sound of birds and cicadas, the flame on the bedspread. *Foom.* The bed explodes and Simon ducks out onto the balcony; the drapes are afire, licking quickly onto the ceiling, and just before he turns to go down the outdoor stairs, Simon sees the fire blackening the mattress.

He walks down the spiral staircase and does not look back until he has nearly crossed the lawn. The birds now seem to be calling out an emergency to one another, and the sun porch is completely engulfed and a dark cloud is rising from the roof, rolling against the sky. His green Mercedes is up here, through this small grove of woods, on the abandoned dirt road.

He drives in a calculated fury down the darkening coast. He has a suitcase in the backseat with clothes and cash; in another car that waits for him in a drugstore parking lot there are more clothes and cash and a number of new identities. After half an hour of driving he gets onto Route 9, controlling his speed a little more carefully; the road winds above cliffs, by cold, majestic homes that are lit against the sky. His headlights sweep over oak, ragged pine trees. Here the road rises; the sea stretches before him, a dark eternity. Here is the dirt pull-off. He slows, and then, where the dirt begins to pitch downward again, he opens the door and *now* goes out shoulder first, rolling, a crack to his head and elbow, scuttling under the scrub brush. Stunned, he watches the Mercedes drift down, picking up speed, toward the guardrail; just yesterday, at eleven at night, he checked that the rail was loose enough not to hold the weight of the car, and the car snaps through easily now. The drivers'-side door swings open as the car bumps over the cliff, taillights blazing, and the vehicle is gone with a heavy, brief explosion of sound. Ghost-Man ducks, for a car whooshes by, lights washing over the trees above where the Mercedes has gone. There are lights on in a mansion high above him, but he doubts he was seen if someone was on the lawn; all they would have noticed, quite distantly, would have been the hesitation of the car and the lights continuing into the trees, then going out. Still, he must quickly get moving.

He raises himself painfully—tests his joints. His arm seems all right. By the time he makes his way to see the car it is almost fully submerged, taillights and green disappearing sluggishly into the waves. He goes back behind cottonwood trees and thickets of sumac and witch hazel, picking his way along the rocky coast— something he practiced yesterday as well—until he is out of eyesight of the mansion. Then he is on the dark highway. Everything seems large and solid, too still, suddenly, after his frenzied evening. A ten-minute walk and he is at an intersection that leads to a small village; the pharmacy is only two miles away. A dog is barking, and the sound and smell of the sea become more distant. There are insects sounding here in the weeds. Ghost-Man walks, watches pale summer homes in the darkness.

Many hours later, at a hotel in Pennsylvania, Ghost-Man gets up and throws sheets aside and does not turn on lights. His arm at the elbow and shoulder is bruised, throbbing. There are rivulets of water light dancing on his shade and ceiling, and he raises the shade and sees what woke him: Someone has turned on the lights of the pool.

He is on the second floor and as he looks down a group of drunks are coming out, laughing, some jumping into the water, and someone—the manager—is admonishing them and the pool light goes out again and what is left is the roof of the hotel, a flag flying, an astonished moon. And the drunks go off to bed and very soon a square light of window just below, across the courtyard, comes on, and the occupants have drawn only lace curtains and Ghost-Man can see a man and a woman, just arrived from the night of revelry, kissing. The woman reaches both arms across, swiftly takes off her dress, then falls on the bed, pulling the man atop her, her legs enveloping him. There is laughter. Ghost-Man watches. His hands grip the windowsill; his eyes remain fixed on the figures below.

NINETEEN

In the darkness behind her lace curtains Tika is being filled, and she lets herself go with Jesse's lovemaking, lets herself scream with it, for Susan is gone and her landlord's bedroom is in the back of the building and it seems as though the darkness is a conspirator, and she loves that she can tease Jesse and make him grow hard and then he can take her like this, and these moments of release. Whenever Susan is here their lovemaking is tense and exciting and quiet, but now she screams with Jesse's thrusting, and it feels that her mouth could not go wider, and when Jesse turns her over she pushes her face into the pillow and takes that cloth with her teeth and feels the rawness of her scream in her throat, her chest, vibrating in her collarbone.

She lies in his arms after, backed up to him, shielded by his lovely nakedness. The faint light from the street comes through the curtains and in a swath across the bed, across the door of the bedroom. The clock beneath her bedside lamp reads 4:05, burning numbers that make her bracelet there, her watch, red as well. The streetlight dims and is blocked for a moment and Tika turns and looks to the window but nothing is there.

She nestles back to Jesse, his thick arm in sleep thrown haphazardly across her breasts. She strokes his forearm, massaging with her fingers the muscles surrounding thumb, strong wrist. In his sleep, he groans. She thinks about the moment she can bring Jesse to, as he makes love; he works for so long that he is exhausted, and then she can say something into his ear, or touch his scrotum, or arc her body toward him and spread her legs a little wider and it is suddenly as if another being in him takes over—this is how it is for her, too—and in that place beyond exhaustion Jesse pushes beyond his pounding heart; he tells her that in orgasm he sees, momentarily, light. Tonight before her own orgasm she saw the circle of Arabian dancers, the spinning veils and gowns and hands; she made a circle of her legs, wrapped them around Jesse, holding him, bringing him into his light.

In a dream later Tika hears the sound of a woman crying with grief. Someone has lost a dog. Who is saying those things? Not Kascha, for Kascha has told Tika many times that she would like a dog, but that with her travel schedule it wouldn't be fair. Such sad, hysterical grief. Tika feels the mattress shifting, Jesse sitting up— that cannot be a dream—but her arms are so heavy and independent that she has not a chance of rising. She senses Jesse's lips on her cheek, hears his voice saying, "I'll check it out, honey." His weight lifts and she thinks she says, *Thank you, sweetie, thanks for taking care of it. Someone is very unhappy.* But she is not sure she's said the words, is almost positive she did not, and Jesse's footsteps creak across the floor and soon she hears him go out the back.

She and Jesse have pulled into a gas station and the landscape around them is barren and as they get out of the car there are a lot of people there looking for a dog. Someone walks on the roof of the station. How the hell would the dog get up there? She wakes to footsteps on the floorboards coming from the back door. She stretches for a moment, anticipating Jesse, and she will ask him about the dog. The dog? Not a dream then, but a woman crying with grief, saying, *"Someone killed my dog,"* and this wakes Tika and there is a man who is not Jesse standing there, looking at her fiercely in this darkness and she screams and his hand is on her mouth and she is struggling, turning, pulling away and the hand is roughly replaced by cloth that smells of gasoline, she is choking on it and her hands are slapping back in terror but the cloth is jerked tighter and she screams in her throat and smells flesh of fist and the man pulls her upright, to get her on her knees, her neck cracking with this force and the voice is saying, "Sshhh, Christ, just listen. Just *listen* to me. I just will tell you, and then you'll know, and I'll be gone, just for once stay still and fucking *listen* —"

Tika reaches and grasps the lamp and swings her arm with it hard, the cord snapping from the wall. She has aimed for the window, but the lamp falls short, ceramic and lightbulb shattering, and the gag tightens fiercely as Tika scrambles, trying to reach the clock, anything that she can throw. *"Goddamnit, fuck,"* the voice is saying, tight and controlled, close to her ear, *"just won't fucking listen."*

Snapping her head back, the man begins to drag Tika off the bed. Still she kicks, tries to get her hands back at him, her fingers into his eyes, listening to the man breathe, horse breaths, and he says, "Oh God, oh my *fuck*ing God"—is he crying?—"now you fucked up everything. I could have just fucking *talked* to you. That's *all*, to make you *see*."

There is rapping, pounding at the front door; Jiri's cane, Jiri is here. Oh, sweet Jiri. "Tika. *Tika*. What is going on? *Open this.*" And there is a hesitation and then Jiri is smashing the glass and the man holding Tika is saying, *"Fuck, fuck, fuck,"* and Tika hears Jesse's voice at the back of the house, pounding on the door there, and the man and the cloth suddenly are gone, a knife, a package of papers sprawling on the floor, and when Tika looks up she sees the figure of the man in her bedroom doorway, his head turned toward the back, for now Jesse is breaking the door open and yelling her name in the hallway, and the man, in that dim light, that heavy smell of fuel everywhere, swivels his head and disappears and bangs through the front door, and Tika looks through the window, and then Jesse is beside her, holding her, and on the porch the man from the darkness and Jiri are grappling, Jiri's white fingers holding the man's waist; in their struggle Tika sees a moment, a glance of Jiri's teeth in the dark.

TWENTY

Jiri has his arms fixed around the waist. There are blows to his head, as if a board is being swung at him repeatedly. He shuts his eyes, hunches his shoulders, squeezes into bone; it is like holding a desperate, wild spider. *Just hang on, goddamnit,* he tells himself, *just don't bloody let him go.*

There is a guttural scream from the man above, a hard cracking behind Jiri's ear.

They are at the edge of the stairs. Then they are falling.

Now there is a heavy sound of crickets in the weeds. Jiri can hear them from where he is, at the foot of Tika's stairs. The medics have just lifted him onto a gurney, an odd, cool feeling of swooping and then solidity, and the blue-white-red lights of police and rescue squads make steady explosions in the leaves nearby. The medics, Jiri realizes, think he is unconscious.

"—doused her place with gasoline and was going to set it on fire," one of them is saying, quietly, as he carefully straps belts about Jiri's torso. "They think he killed someone in Medford to-night, and that he was the one, like a year ago, who murdered those two women a few miles away in Somerville and burned them in their houses—"

A black man above Jiri, gently fitting foam about Jiri's head, gives a low whistle. "God forbid. I remember that. These people are lucky." Jiri sees the dark skin, nostrils, large hands moving.

"This guy, here," says the first medic, "he held him until the boyfriend and the police came." Then, realizing Jiri's eyes are open, he says more loudly, "Hey, fella. Rest easy. You're quite a guy. You're gonna be okay. How are you feeling?"

But Jiri cannot speak. The eyes of the medic show a quick con-cern, and then the face is smiling again. "Just rest easy, fella."

But there is something I need to know, Jiri tries to say. It comes out a moan. *Goddamnit.* Now Anna's sweet head is above him, against the lights of Tika's house, and her head lowers and she is kissing his fingers. And Jiri wants to tell her not to worry but the words do not come; he tells himself to be patient and just then his father is here, on the other side, holding Jiri's other hand. Behind his father's form Trowbridge Street is a spectacular jungle of the leaves and red light of the fire trucks, the crackling of police dispatches. *What is this place, Jiri?* his father says. His father is in silhouette against the red, and when Jiri cannot answer him, he presses Jiri's fingers as if in prayer. It is so startling—so breathtaking—to see his father that Jiri feels he will weep and tries to raise his head but he cannot move it.

One of the medics is telling Anna that she can ride with him and they are making sure his head is stabilized and the gurney is moving now, branches running above, and Jiri wonders where Tika is, but when they raise the gurney, a strong clicking of metal, he can see that she is right here, where his father was, saying, "Jiri, oh,

Jiri," and she is all right, and *That is what I needed to know.* The musician with the glasses is behind her, holding her shoulders, good boy. The boy was tough and fought with the man when Jiri no longer could.

The raising of Jiri's body brings the cool sensation again and there is pain in his head and neck. They take in the legs of the gurney, and trees over Jiri are sliding, becoming the white ambulance ceiling.

"We'll meet you guys there," Tika says.

"Yes, honey," Anna says.

Jiri feels suddenly that his back is horribly strained and he tries to say so and Anna is next to him and there is a sharp smell of alcohol and Jiri sees the medic looking at Anna. Then the doors close; they become a distant pair of windows, distant leaves glittering, vibrant—*is he a boy, looking at the leaves of Bohemia?*

Anna speaks in Czech to him, very close, and far beneath them the wheels of the ambulance roll, moving over the familiar surface of Trowbridge Street. Streetlights whisk through the windows, then steady in a turn, and the ambulance accelerates again, the siren starting up, and they are on Cambridge Avenue, rushing fast through the September morning, Anna holding Jiri's hand tight between her own.

ACKNOWLEDGMENTS

I would like to express my gratitude to my editor, John Parsley, for his empathy and patience and wise eye, and my agent, Maria Massie, of Lippincott Massie McQuilkin, for helping put these pages into print.

I was blessed in the revising of this book by Carl Beckman, Kerrie Clapp, Richard Fleischer, Emily Hamilton, Jack Herlihy, Stacy Howe, Ruth and Josef Hůrka, Kristin Livingston, Linda Martin, Sean McKenna, Conan McKye, Mark Morelli, Cristina Mueller, Marwa Othman, Carol Thomas, Enid Thuermer, Frank Reeve, Věra Šperl, Freddy Sullivan, and librarians at the Tucker Free Library in Henniker, New Hampshire, including Helga Winn, Lori Roukey, Betty Rood, and Jill Stearns. Ken DeStasio, a speech language pathologist at the Rutland Regional Medical Center in Rutland, Vermont, helped me determine the course of this story, and we lost him far too early. All of these people helped me with research, read my work in progress, and gave me hope.

Others, in a very difficult time, gave me the strength to keep going with this manuscript and lifted me onto their shoulders: Bill

Cantwell, the family Dubus, Margit and Wayne France, Matt Miller and my brother, Christopher Jan Hurka, and his family—Caryn, Ian, Nick, and Noel. Dr. Montford (Bunny) Sayce has somehow kept his faith in his student all of these years.

I thank Dr. Peter Paicos and his team at the Winchester Wound Center in Medford, Massachusetts, and the administrators, nurses, and medical teams at Winchester Hospital in Winchester, Massachusetts, for their unfailing kindness to my family and my father.

Dr. Jerome (Jerry) Zacks, of Mount Sinai Hospital in New York City, was a true angel of mercy for my family and gave my father extra time with his loved ones. Heather Heckman-McKenna kept close watch on my heart—thank you so much, wonderful Heather. Ellen Nickel-Stone held me and showed me the stars.

And my father, Josef Hůrka, worked tirelessly on this book with me until he went to those stars—revising, translating, making sure of the accuracy of the work, particularly regarding intelligence and Resistance information. So Dad, thank you, as always: We are forever soldiers together.

J. H.